D0343697

# Stranded in His Arms

*Falling in love in the face of danger!*

As the water level rises in a Somerset village ambulance partners Mimi Sawyer and Jack Halliday race towards a pregnant woman fast approaching her due date. But when a river bursts its banks this fearless team is separated, and Mimi and Jack find themselves facing the strongest challenge yet to the walls around their hearts…!

Don't miss this exciting new duet by

**Annie Claydon**

Mimi and Rafe's story
*Rescued by Dr Rafe*

and

Jack and Cass's story
*Saved by the Single Dad*

Available now!

Dear Reader,

When I started to write *Saved by the Single Dad* I knew that my heroine was going to be a bit special—so she needed a special name. And when I settled on one it meant a phone call to one of my friends—did she mind if I appropriated her name for my heroine? The real Cassandra rather liked the idea that the fictional Cassandra would be six feet tall, flame-haired and able to lift the hero off his feet, and so my heroine was born. She's very different from my friend, but in my eyes they have one thing in common. They're both true heroines.

Of course a heroine like this needs a special hero. Many men would be challenged by Cass's do-anything attitude but Jack loves it—which is precisely what I like about him.

Thank you for reading Jack and Cass's story. I always enjoy hearing from readers, and you can contact me via my website at annieclaydon.com.

*Annie* x

# SAVED BY THE SINGLE DAD

BY
ANNIE CLAYDON

® and TM are trademarks owned and used by the trademark owner
and/or its licensee. Trademarks marked with ® are registered with the
United Kingdom Patent Office and/or the Office for Harmonisation in
the Internal Market and in other countries.

Published in Great Britain 2016
By Mills & Boon, an imprint of HarperCollins*Publishers*
1 London Bridge Street, London, SE1 9GF

© 2016 Annie Claydon

ISBN: 978-0-263-06534-3

Our policy is to use papers that are natural, renewable and recyclable
products and made from wood grown in sustainable forests. The logging
and manufacturing processes conform to the legal environmental
regulations of the country of origin.

Printed and bound in Great Britain
by CPI Antony Rowe, Chippenham, Wiltshire

Cursed with a poor sense of direction and a propensity to read, **Annie Claydon** spent much of her childhood lost in books. A degree in English Literature followed by a career in computing didn't lead directly to her perfect job—writing romance for Mills & Boon—but she has no regrets in taking the scenic route. She lives in London: a city where getting lost can be a joy.

### Books by Annie Claydon

### Mills & Boon Medical Romance

*The Doctor Meets Her Match*
*The Rebel and Miss Jones*
*Re-awakening His Shy Nurse*
*Once Upon a Christmas Night...*
*200 Harley Street: The Enigmatic Surgeon*
*A Doctor to Heal Her Heart*
*Snowbound with the Surgeon*
*Daring to Date Her Ex*
*The Doctor She'd Never Forget*
*Discovering Dr Riley*

Visit the Author Profile page at millsandboon.co.uk for more titles.

For the real Cassandra

# CHAPTER ONE

JACK PUT HIS head down, trying to shield his face from the stinging rain. Behind him, his ambulance was parked on the road, unable to make it across the narrow bridge that was now the only way into the small village of Holme. Ahead of him, a heavily pregnant woman who should be transported to hospital before the late summer floods in this area of Somerset got any worse.

He and Mimi had been in worse situations before. They'd crewed an ambulance together for the last seven years, Mimi in the driver's seat and Jack taking the lead in treating their patients. They were a good team.

But, however good they were, they couldn't stop it from raining. The main road to the hilltop village was under three feet of water and this back road led across a narrow bridge that was slick with mud. Rather than risk the ambulance getting stuck halfway across, they'd decided to make the rest of the journey on foot.

There were still plenty of options. The patient wasn't in labour yet, and maybe a four-by-four could bring her down the hill to the waiting ambulance. Maybe the storm would clear and the HEMS team could airlift her out. Maybe the support doctor Jack had requested would arrive soon, and maybe not. If all else failed, he and Mimi had delivered babies together before now.

His feet slid on a patch of mud and he gripped the heavy medical bag slung over his shoulder, lurching wildly for a moment before he regained his balance. 'Careful...' He muttered the word as an instruction to himself. Slipping and breaking his leg wasn't one of the options he had been considering.

'One, two, three...' In a grim version of the stepping game he played with Ellie, his four-year-old daughter, he traversed the bridge, trying to ignore the grumbling roar of thunder in the hills. He'd wait for Mimi on the far bank of the river. She'd walked back up the road a little to get reception on her phone and check in with the Disaster Control Team, but they shouldn't lose sight of each other.

He thought he heard someone scream his name but it was probably just the screech of the wind. Then, as the roar got louder, he realised that it wasn't thunder.

Jack turned. A wall of water, tumbling down from the hills, was travelling along the path of the riverbed straight towards him.

His first instinct was to trust the power and speed of his body and run, but in a moment of sudden clarity he knew he wouldn't make it up the steep muddy path in front of him in time. A sturdy-looking tree stood just yards away, its four twisting trunks offering some hope of protection, and Jack dropped his bag and ran towards it.

He barely had a chance to lock his hands around one of the trunks and suck in one desperate breath before the water slammed against his back, expelling all of the precious oxygen from his lungs in one gasp as it flattened him against the bark. A great roar deafened him and he kept his eyes tight shut against the water and grit hitting his face. *Hang on.* The one and only thing he could do was hang on.

Then it stopped. Not daring to let go of the tree trunk,

Jack opened his eyes, trying to blink away the sting of the dirty water. Another sickening roar was coming from upstream.

The next wave was bigger, tearing at his body. He tried to hold on but his fingers slipped apart and he was thrown against the other three trunks, one of them catching the side of his head with a dizzying blow. There was no point in trying to hold his breath and a harsh bellow escaped his lips as his arms flailed desperately, finding something to hold on to and clinging tight.

Then, suddenly, it stopped again. Too dazed to move, Jack lay twisted in the shelter of the branches, his limbs trembling with shock and effort. He was so cold…

*Mimi*… He tried to call for her, hoping against all hope that she hadn't been on the bridge when the water had hit, but all he could do was cough and retch, dirty water streaming out of his nose and mouth.

He gasped in a lungful of air. 'Mimi…'

'Stay down. Just for a moment.'

A woman's voice, husky and sweet. Someone was wiping his face, clearing his eyes and mouth.

'Mimi… My partner.'

'She's okay. I can see her on the other side of the river.' That voice again. He reached out towards it and felt a warm hand grip his.

He opened his eyes, blinking against the light, and saw her face. Pale skin, with strands of short red hair escaping from the hood of her jacket. Strong cheekbones, a sweet mouth and the most extraordinary pale blue eyes. It was the kind of face you'd expect to find on some warrior goddess…

He shook his head. He must be in shock. Jack knew better than most the kind of nonsense that people babbled in situations like this. Unless she had a golden sword tucked away under her dark blue waterproof jacket, she was just an ordinary mortal, her face rendered ethereal because it was the first thing he'd seen when he opened his eyes.

'Are you sure? Mimi's okay?'

The woman glanced up only briefly, her gaze returning to him. 'She's wearing an ambulance service jacket. Blonde hair, I think…'

'Yes, that's her.' Jack tried to move and found that his limbs had some strength in them now.

'Are you hurt?'

'No…' No one part of him hurt any more than the rest and Jack decided that was a good sign. 'Thanks…um…'

'I'm Cass… Cassandra Clarke.'

'Jack Halliday.'

She gave a small nod in acknowledgement. 'We'd better not hang around here for too long. Can you stand?'

'Yeah.'

'Okay, take it slowly.' She reached over, disentangling his foot from a branch, and then scrambled around next to him, squeezing her body in between him and one of the tree trunks. With almost no effort on his part at all, he found himself sitting up as she levered her weight against his, her arms supporting him. Then she helped him carefully to his feet.

He turned, looking back over the bridge to find Mimi. Only the bridge wasn't there any more. A couple of chunks of masonry were all that was left of it, rolling downstream under the pressure of the boiling water. He could see Mimi standing on the other side, staring fixedly at him, and beside her stood a man who he thought he recognised. Behind them, the lights still on and the driver's door open, was a black SUV.

'All right?' Now that he was on his feet, he could see that Cass was tall, just a couple of inches shorter than him.

'Yeah. Thanks.' Jack felt for his phone and found that

he had nothing in his pocket apart from a couple of stones and a handful of sludge. 'I need to get to a phone...'

'Okay. The village is only ten minutes away; we'll get you up there first.' She spoke with a quiet, irresistible authority.

Jack waved to Mimi, feeling a sharp ache in his shoulder as he raised his arm. She waved back, both hands reaching out towards him as if she was trying to retrieve him. Moving his hand in a circular motion as a sign that he'd call her, he saw the man bend to pick something up. Mimi snatched her phone from him and looked at it for a moment and then turned her attention back on to Jack, sending him a thumbs-up sign.

'Did you mean to park the ambulance like that?' There was a note of dry humour in Cass's husky tones.

Jack looked over the water and saw that the ambulance had been washed off the road and was leaning at a precarious angle against a tree. He muttered a curse under his breath.

'I'll take that as a no.'

Jack chuckled, despite the pain in his ribs. 'What are you?'

She flushed red as if this was the one question she didn't know how to answer. In someone so capable, the delicate shade of pink on her cheeks stirred his shaking limbs into sudden warmth.

'What do you mean?'

'None of this fazes you very much, does it? And you've been trained in how to lift...' Jack recognised the techniques she'd used as very similar to his own. A little more leverage and a little less strength, maybe. And, although Cass didn't give any orders, the men around her seemed to recognise her as their leader.

'I'm a firefighter. I work at the fire station in town, but I'm off duty at the moment. On duty as a concerned family member, though—my sister Lynette's the patient you're coming to see.'

'Then we'd better get going.' Jack looked around for his bag and saw that one of the men was holding it, and that water was dripping out of it. He really was on his own here—no Mimi and no medical bag. He turned, accepting a supportive arm from one of the men, and began to walk slowly up the steep path with the group.

This wasn't what Cass had planned. She'd hoped to be able to get Lynette safely to hospital well in advance but, stubborn as ever, her sister had pointed out that it was another two weeks before her due date and flatly refused to go.

The hospital was now out of reach, but a paramedic was the next best thing. And the floods had finally given her a break and quite literally washed Jack up, on to her doorstep.

Despite the layers of clothing, she'd still felt the strength of his body when she'd helped him up. Hard muscle, still pumped and quivering with the effort of holding on. It had taken nerve to stay put and hang on instead of trying to run from the water, but that decision had probably saved his life.

He was tall as well, a couple of inches taller than her own six feet. And despite, or maybe because of, all that raw power he had the gentlest eyes. The kind of deep brown that a girl could just fall into.

Enough. He might be easy on the eye, but that was nothing to do with her primary objective. Jack was walking ahead of her and Cass lengthened her stride to catch up with him.

'Lynette's actually been having mild contractions. She's not due for another two weeks, but it seems as if the baby might come sooner.' It was better to think of him as an asset, someone who could help her accomplish the task ahead. Bravery had got him here in one piece and those tender eyes might yet come in useful, for comforting Lynette.

'Her first child?'

'Yes.' And one that Cass would protect at all costs.

'Hopefully it'll decide not to get its feet wet just yet. The weather's too bad for the HEMS team to be able to operate safely tonight, but we may be able to airlift her out in the morning.'

'Thanks. You'll contact them?'

'Yeah. Can I borrow your phone? I need to get hold of Mimi as well.'

'Of course, but we'll get you inside first. Who's the guy with her?'

'If it's who I think it is, that's her ex.' A brief grin. Brief but very nice. 'Mimi's not going to like *him* turning up out of the blue.'

'Complicated?'

'Isn't it always?'

He had a point. In any given situation, the complications always seemed to far outweigh the things that went right. Which meant that someone as gorgeous as Jack was probably dizzyingly complicated.

'She'll be okay, though? Your partner.'

'Oh, yeah. No problems with Rafe; he won't leave her stranded. He might have to tie her to a tree to stop her from killing him, but she'll be okay.' Despite the fact that Jack was visibly shivering, the warmth in his eyes was palpable.

Maybe Cass should have done that with *her* ex, Paul. Tied him to a tree and killed him when she'd had the chance. But he was a father now, and probably a half decent one at that. He had a new wife, and a child who depended on him.

'I don't suppose there's any way we can get some more medical supplies over here?' Jack's voice broke her reverie. 'Rafe's a doctor and, knowing him, he'll have come prepared for anything. I could do with a few things, just in case.'

Cass nodded. 'Leave it with me; I'll work something out. You need to get cleaned up and into some dry clothes before you do anything else.'

'Yeah.' The tremble of his limbs was making it through into Jack's voice now. 'I could do with a hot shower.'

'That's exactly where we're headed. Church hall.'

'That's where we're staying tonight?' He looked towards the spire, which reached up into the sky ahead of them like a beacon at the top of the hill.

'Afraid so. The water's already pretty deep all around the village. In this storm, and with the flash floods, there's no safe place to cross.'

She could count on the water keeping him here for the next twenty-four hours at least, perhaps more if she was lucky. He might not want to stay, but there was no choice.

'I'm not thinking of trying to get across. Not while I have a patient to tend to.'

'Thank you. I really appreciate that.' Cass felt suddenly ashamed of herself. This guy wasn't an asset, a cog in a piece of machinery. He was a living, breathing man and his dedication to his job wasn't taken out of a rule book.

She reminded herself, yet again, that this kind of thinking would only get her into trouble. Paul had left her because she'd been unable to get pregnant. Then told her that the problem was all hers, proving his point by becoming a father seven months later. In the agony of knowing that she might never have the baby she so wanted, the indignity of the timing was almost an afterthought.

That was all behind her. The tearing disappointment each month. The wedding, which Paul had postponed time and time again and had ended up cancelled. Lynette's baby was the one she had to concentrate on now, and she was going to fight tooth and nail to get everything that her sister needed.

\* \* \*

Jack was taking one thing at a time. He fixed his eyes on the church steeple, telling himself that this was the goal for the time being and that he just had to cajole his aching limbs into getting there.

Slowly it rose on the horizon, towering dizzily above his head as they got closer. The church had evidently been here for many hundreds of years but, when Cass led him around the perimeter of the grey, weatherworn stones, the building behind it was relatively new. She walked through a pair of swing doors into a large lobby filled with racks of coats. At the far end, shadows passed to and fro behind a pair of obscure glass doors, which obviously led to the main hall.

'The showers are through here.' Cass indicated a door at the side of the lobby.

'Wait.' There was one thing he needed to do, and then he'd leave the rest to Cass and hope that the water was hot. 'Give me your phone.'

She hesitated. 'The medical bags can wait. You need to get warm.'

'Won't take a minute.' He held out his hand, trying not to wince as pain shot through his shoulders and Cass nodded, producing her phone from her pocket.

'Thank you. Tell her that we're going back down to fetch the medical supplies. I think I know how we can get them across.'

It didn't come as any particular surprise that she had a plan. Jack imagined that Cass was the kind of person who always had a plan. She was tall and strong, and moved with the controlled grace of someone who knew how to focus on the task in hand. Now that she'd pulled her hood back her thick red hair, cut in a layered style that was both practical and feminine, made her seem even more gorgeously formidable.

His text to Mimi was answered immediately and confirmed that it was Rafe that he'd seen. Jack texted again, asking Mimi to pack whatever spare medical supplies they had into a bag.

'Here.' He passed the phone back to Cass. 'She's waiting for your call.'

'Thanks.' She slipped the phone into her pocket. 'Now you get warm.'

She led the way through to a large kitchen, bustling with activity, which suddenly quieted as they tramped through in their muddy boots and wet clothes. Beyond that, a corridor led to a bathroom, with a sign saying 'Women Only' hung on the door. Cass popped her head inside and then flipped the sign over, to display the words 'Men Only'.

It looked as if he had the place to himself. There was a long row of handbasins, neat and shining, with toilet cubicles lined up opposite and bath and shower cubicles at the far end. The place smelled of bleach and air freshener.

'Put your clothes there.' She indicated a well-scrubbed plastic chair next to the handbasins. 'I'll send someone to collect them and leave some fresh towels and we'll find some dry clothes. What size are you…?'

The question was accompanied by a quick up and down glance that made Jack shiver, and a slight flush spread over Cass's cheeks. 'Large will have to do, I think.' She made the words sound like a compliment.

'Thanks. That would be great.'

'Do you need any help?' She looked at him steadily. 'I'm relying on you, as a medical professional, to tell me if there's anything the matter with you.'

If he'd thought for one moment that Cass would stay and help him off with his clothes, instead of sending someone else in to do it, Jack might just have said yes. 'No. I'll be fine.'

'Good.' She turned quickly, but Jack caught sight of a half-smile on her lips. Maybe she would have stayed.

Working in an environment that was still predominantly male, Jack doubted that she was much fazed by the sight of a man's body.

He waited for the door to close behind her before he painfully took off his jacket and sweater. Unbuttoning his shirt, he stood in front of the mirror to inspect some of the damage. It was impossible to tell what was what at the moment. A little blood, mixed with a great deal of mud from the dirty water. He'd shower first and then worry about any bumps and scratches.

A knock at the door and a woman's voice, asking if she could come in, disturbed the best shower Jack could remember taking in a long time. Hurried footsteps outside the cubicle and then he was alone again, luxuriating in the hot water.

After soaping his body twice, he felt almost clean again. Opening the cubicle door a crack, he peered out and found the bathroom empty; two fluffy towels hung over one of the handbasins. One was large enough to wind around his waist and he rubbed the other one over his head to dry his hair.

He looked a mess. He could feel a bump forming on the side of his head and, although his jacket had largely protected the rest of him, he had friction burns on his arms, which stung like crazy, and a graze on his chest from where the zip on his jacket had been driven against the skin.

'Coming in...' A rap on the door and a man's voice. A slim, sandy-haired man of about forty entered, carrying a pile of clothes and a pair of canvas shoes. 'Hi, Jack. I'm Martin.'

He was wearing a light windcheater, white letters on a dark blue background on the right hand side, in the same place that Jack's paramedic insignia appeared on his uniform. When he turned, the word was repeated in larger letters across his back.

'You're the vicar, then.' Jack grinned.

'Yeah. My wife seems to think this is a good idea, just in case anyone mistakes me for someone useful.'

'I'd always be glad to see you coming.' Hope and comfort were often just as important as medical treatment.

'Likewise. We're grateful for all you did to get here.' Martin propped the clothes on the ledge behind the washbasins. 'They look nasty.' His gaze was on the friction burns on Jack's arms.

'Superficial. They'll be okay.' Jack riffled through the clothes. A T-shirt, a grey hooded sweatshirt and a pair of jeans that looked about his size. He picked the T-shirt up and pulled it over his head so that he didn't have to think about the marks on his arms and chest any more. 'How's my patient?'

'Lynette's fine. She's over at the vicarage, drinking tea with my wife and complaining about all the fuss. She seems to have got it into her head that she's got some say about when the baby arrives.'

'You were right to call. At the very least she needs to be checked over.'

Martin nodded. 'Thanks. Cass has gone to get your medical supplies. Goodness only knows how she's going to manage it, but knowing Cass…'

Even the mention of her name made Jack's heart beat a little faster. 'She seems very resourceful.'

Martin nodded. 'Yeah. Bit too resourceful sometimes. Now, important question. Tea or coffee? I don't think I can keep the Monday Club under control for much longer.'

Jack chuckled. 'Tea. Milk, no sugar, thanks.'

'Good. And I hope you like flapjacks or I'm going to have a riot on my hands.'

'You seem very organised here.'

Martin nodded. 'This church has been taking people in for the last eight hundred years. Wars, famine, fires… Now floods. I've never seen anything like this, though, and I've been here fifteen years. Half the village is flooded out.'

'How many people do you have here?'

'Just a couple of families staying overnight. We've found everyone else billets in people's homes. But everyone eats here, and we have an action committee...' Martin shrugged, grinning. 'That's Cass's baby. I confine myself to tea and sympathy.'

Jack reckoned that Martin was downplaying his own considerable role. 'And hospitality.'

'We've never turned anyone away before, and that's not going to start on my watch.' A trace of determination broke through Martin's affable smile and was quickly hidden. 'Anything else you need?'

'A phone? I'd like to call home.'

'Yes, of course. The landline at the vicarage is still working; you can use that.' Martin turned, making for the door. 'Come to the kitchen when you're ready and I'll take you over there.'

# CHAPTER TWO

MARTIN OPENED A side door that led out of the kitchen and they walked along a paved path, sheltered by makeshift awnings that boasted a few scraps of soggy coloured bunting hanging from the corners. Then through a gate and into the vicarage kitchen, which oozed warmth and boasted a table large enough to seat a dozen people.

Lynette was red-haired like her sister, her features prettier and yet somehow far less attractive. She was heavily pregnant and Jack's first impressions were that she was in the best of health. Although she'd been having minor contractions, she seemed stubbornly positive that the baby wasn't coming yet. Jack begged to differ, but kept that thought to himself.

He left Lynette on the sofa by the kitchen range and sat down at the table, where a cup of tea was waiting for him. 'I'll be able to examine you a little more thoroughly when your sister gets back with my medical bag.'

'Thanks. But there's really no need to worry. First babies are always late, aren't they?'

Sue, the vicar's wife, frowned. 'Not necessarily. My Josh was early.' She pushed a large plate of flapjacks across the table towards Jack. 'If I eat another one of those I'll be sorry when I get on the scales. I wish the Monday Club would stop cooking…'

Lynette laughed. 'Not much chance of that. Mrs Hawes doesn't like to see anyone going hungry.'

Sue sighed, looking up as someone rapped on the glass pane of the back door. 'It's open...'

The door swung inwards and two bags were placed inside. Then Cass appeared, her hair wet and slicked back from her face, holding her muddy boots in one hand and her wet jacket and overtrousers in the other. Sue relieved her of them and disappeared to put them in the front porch.

'You got two across?' Jack bent to inspect the contents of the bags.

'Yeah, we got a line over about quarter of a mile down from the bridge. Mimi's okay and she's going back to the hospital with what's-his-name.' The corners of her mouth quirked into an expression that would have been unfathomable if Jack hadn't been able to guess the situation. 'She sends you her love.'

Jack nodded, drawing a stethoscope and blood pressure monitor from the bag. 'Right, ladies. If you're comfortable here, Lynette, I'll get on and do a more thorough examination.'

He'd given Lynette one last flash of those tender eyes and smiled at her, pronouncing that everything was fine. Lynette hadn't even noticed what he hadn't said, but Cass had.

'She's in the early stages of labour, isn't she?' Cass had shown him through to the small room behind the church hall, which had been earmarked as his sleeping quarters and already boasted a hastily erected camp bed in the corner, with sheets and blankets folded on top of it.

'Yes. Although this could be a false alarm...'

Another thing he wasn't saying. 'And it might not be.'

'Yes.' He scrubbed his hand back across his scalp, his short dark hair spiking untidily. 'I have everything I need, and I've delivered babies plenty of times before.'

'Really?' Jack was saying everything she wanted to hear, and Cass wondered how much of it was just reassurance.

'It's not ideal, but we'll get her to the hospital as soon as the weather lifts. In the meantime, you've done your job and you can rely on me to do mine.'

A small curl of warmth quieted some of the fear. 'Thanks. This baby is...' Important. All babies were important, but this one was important to her.

'I know. And he's going to be fine.' His eyes made her believe it. 'Is the father on the scene?'

'Very much so. He's not here, though; Lynette's husband is in the Royal Navy and he's away at the moment. My father works abroad too; Mum was going to come home next week to help out.'

'So it's just you and me then.' He contrived to make that sound like a good thing. 'You're her birth partner?'

'Yep.' Cass pressed her lips together. Going to classes with Lynette had seemed like the most natural thing in the world. The most beautiful form of sharing between sisters. Now it was all terrifying.

'Good.' His gaze chipped away at yet another piece of the fear that had been laying heavy on her chest for days, and suddenly Cass wondered if she might not make a half decent job of it after all.

'I'd rather be...' Anything. 'I'd rather be doing something practical.'

He laughed. 'This is the most practical thing in the world, Cass. The one thing that never changes, and hopefully never will. You'll both be fine.'

She knew that he was trying to reassure her, and that his *You'll both be fine* wasn't a certainty, but somehow it seemed to be working. She walked over to the coil of ropes and pulleys that had been dumped here while she'd taken the bags through to the vicarage.

'I'll get these out of your way.'

'Let me help you.' Before she could stop him, he'd picked up the rope, leaving Cass to collect the remaining pulleys and carabiners up and put them into a rucksack. 'You used this to get the bags across?'

'Yeah.' Hopefully he was too busy thinking about child-birth to take much notice of what he was carrying. The cut end was clearly visible, hanging from the coil of rope. 'I borrowed the gear from one of the guys in the village who goes mountaineering.' She slung the rucksack over her shoulder and led the way through to the storeroom, indicating an empty patch of floor, but Jack shook his head.

'Not there; it's too close to the radiator and rope degrades if it dries out too fast. Help me move these boxes and we'll lay it flat over here.'

Cass dumped the rucksack and started to lift the boxes out of the way. 'You know something about rope?'

'Enough to know that this one's been cut recently, while it was under stress. Mountaineering ropes don't just break.' He bent to finger the cut end and then turned his gaze on to her.

The security services had missed a trick in not recruiting Jack and putting him to work as an interrogator. Those quiet eyes made it impossible not to admit to her greatest follies. 'I…cut the rope.'

Somehow that wasn't enough. He didn't even need to ask; Cass found herself needing to tell him the rest.

'Mimi shouted across, asking if we had a harness. They both seemed determined to try and get across, and medical bags are one thing…'

'But lives are another?' he prompted her gently.

'Yeah. I was worried that they'd just go ahead and do it, and as soon as one of them put their weight on the ropes I wouldn't be able to stop them. So, when we got hold of the second bag, I cut the rope.'

He grinned. 'I couldn't see Mimi letting you haul a bag over and staying put herself on the other side. Nice job.'

Cass supposed she might as well tell him everything; he'd hear it soon enough. 'Not such a nice job. I miscalculated and the rope snapped back in their direction. Another few feet and it would have taken Mimi's head off.'

'It was…what, thirty feet across the river?'

'About that.'

'Weight of the bags…' He was obviously doing some kind of calculation in his head. 'Wouldn't have taken her head off. Maybe given her a bit of a sting.'

'Well, it frightened the life out of me. And what's-his-name…'

'Rafe…'

'Yeah, Rafe tackled her to the ground.'

Jack snorted with laughter. 'Oh, I'll bet she just loved that. Rafe always was a bit on the protective side where Mimi's concerned.'

'She didn't seem too pleased about it. What is it with those two? Light the blue touchpaper?'

'Yeah and stand a long way back.' Jack was still chuckling. 'Shame, really. They're both good people, but put them within fifty feet of each other and they're a disaster. Always will be.'

'I know the feeling…' All too well. Only Cass would be a disaster with any man. She'd never quite been able to move on from what Paul had said and done, never been able to shake the belief that he was right. She'd felt her heart close, retreating wounded from a world that had been too painful to bear.

He didn't reply. As Jack bent to finish arranging the ropes so they'd dry out properly, Cass couldn't help noticing the strong lines of his body, the ripple of muscle. That didn't just happen; it must have taken some hard work and training.

'So you're a mountaineer?'

He shook his head, not looking at her. 'No. My father. It's not something I'd ever consider doing.'

That sounded far too definite not to be a thought-out decision. 'Too risky?' Somehow Cass doubted that; Jack had just braved a flood to get here.

'There's risk and risk. My father died when I was twelve, free climbing. Anyone with an ounce of sanity would have used ropes for that particular climb, but he went for the adrenaline high. He always did.' The sudden bitter anger in Jack's voice left Cass in no doubt about his feelings for his father.

'I'm really sorry...'

He straightened up. 'Long time ago. It was one of the things that made me want to go into frontline medicine. Going out on a limb to save a life has always seemed to me to be a much finer thing than doing it for kicks.'

'And of course we both calculate the risks we take pretty carefully.' Cass wondered whether Jack knew that the current calculation was all about him. She wanted to know more about the man who was responsible for Lynette's safety, to gauge his weaknesses.

He nodded. 'Yeah. Needs a cool head, not a hot one.'

Good answer. Cass turned to the door. 'Shall we go and see whether there's any more tea going?'

They collected their tea from an apparently unending supply in the kitchen, and Jack followed Cass as she dodged the few steps into the back of the church building. She led him along a maze of silent corridors and through a doorway, so small that they both had to duck to get through it.

They were in a closed porch. Arched wooden doors led through to the church on one side and on the other a second door was secured by heavy metal bolts. Tall, stone-framed windows, glazed in a diamond pattern of small pieces of glass, so old that they were almost opaque. A gargoyle, perched up in a corner, grinned down at them.

'I reckoned you might like to drink your tea in peace.' She reached up to switch on a battery-operated lantern, which hung from one of the stone scrolls which flanked the doorway. 'Martin's lent me this place for the duration. I come here to think.'

It looked more like somewhere to hide than think. Jack wondered why she should need such a place when she was clearly surrounded by family and friends here. She seemed so involved with her community, so trusted, and yet somehow she held herself apart from it.

All the same, for some reason she'd let him in and it felt like too much of a privilege to question it. Jack took his jacket off and sat down on one of the stone benches that ran the length of the porch. She proffered a cushion, from a pile hidden away in an alcove in the corner, and he took it gratefully.

'You've made yourself at home here. It's warm as well. And oddly peaceful.' Jack looked around. Listening to the storm outside, rather than struggling against it, made the old walls seem like a safe cocoon.

'I like it. These stones are so thick it's always the same temperature, winter or summer.' She laid her coat out on the bench and smoothed her half-dried hair behind her ears.

'Makes a good refuge.' He smiled, in an indication that she could either take the observation seriously or pass it off as a joke if she chose.

'Yeah. You should ask Martin about that; he's a bit of a history buff. Apparently there was an incident during the English Civil War when Cavaliers claimed refuge here. They camped out in this porch for weeks.'

Fair enough. So she didn't want to talk about it.

'I'd like you to stay with Lynette tonight, at the vicarage. Keep an eye on her.'

She nodded. 'I don't have much choice. My house is a little way downriver from the bridge. It was partially flooded even before this afternoon.'

'I'm sorry to hear that.'

Cass leaned back, stretching her legs out in front of her. 'I've been expecting it for days and at least I had a chance to get everything upstairs, which is a lot more than some people have had. It's my own stupid fault, anyway.'

'So you're the one, are you? That's been making it rain.'

She really was stunningly beautiful when she smiled. Warm and beautiful, actually, with a touch of vulnerability that belied her matter-of-fact attitude and her capable do-anything frame. But she seemed far too ready to blame herself when things went wrong.

'I wish. Then I could make it stop. The house has been in my family for generations and it's always been safe from flooding.'

'But not on your watch?' Jack realised he'd hit a nerve from the slight downward quirk of her lips.

'There used to be a drystone wall, banked up on the inside, which acted as a barrier between the house and the river. My grandparents levelled a stretch of it to give easy access to build an extension at the back. When they died they left the house to Lynette and me and, as she and Steven already had a place up in the village, I bought her out. I was pretty stretched for cash and thought I couldn't afford to reinstate the wall for a few years. Turns out I couldn't afford not to.'

'You're being a bit hard on yourself, aren't you? I'd be devastated if my place were flooded.'

Cass shrugged. 'I'm concentrating on Lynette and the baby. Bricks and mortar can wait.'

Jack nodded, sipping his tea.

'So how about you?' She seemed intent on changing the subject now. 'You have children?'

'A little girl. Ellie's four.'

She smiled. 'That's nice. I'm sorry we're keeping you away from her.'

If he was honest, he was sorry about that too. Jack knew exactly what it was like to have to come to terms with the idea that his father was never coming back, and he'd promised Ellie that he would always come back for her. Right now the storm and the floods made that impossible, and the feeling that he was letting Ellie down was eating at him.

Cass didn't need to know that. 'I'm concentrating on Lynette and the baby too.' He received a bright grin in acknowledgement of the sentiment. 'I'd really like to call my daughter to say goodnight, though. Would you mind if I borrowed your phone?'

'Yes, of course.' She stood up, handing her phone over. 'I'll leave you to it.'

'That's okay. Say hello to her.'

She hesitated and then sat back down with a bump. Awkwardly, she pointed to one of the icons on the small screen.

'You could try a video call. She might like to see you.'

'Yeah, she would. Thanks.'

Jack couldn't remember his sister's mobile number so he called the landline, repeating Cass's mobile number over to Sarah. 'My sister's going to get back to us.'

'Your wife works too?'

'I'm a single father. Sarah has a boy of Ellie's age and she looks after her when I'm working.'

'Sounds like a good arrangement.' She seemed to be getting more uncomfortable by the minute. If he hadn't already come to the conclusion that Cass could deal with almost anything, he would have said she was flustered.

He didn't have time to question why because the phone rang. Cass leaned over, jabbing an icon on the screen to switch on the camera and answer the call.

* * *

He was so in love with Ellie. Cass had reckoned that a wife and family would put Jack firmly out of bounds, which was the best place for him as far as she was concerned. But he was handsome, caring, funny...*and single*. She was going to have to work a little harder now, because allowing herself to be tempted by Jack was just an exercise in loss.

*'Daddeee!'* An excited squeal came from the phone and Cass averted her gaze. Jack held the phone out in front of him, his features softening into a grin that made her want to run away screaming.

'Ellie! What are you up to, darling?'

'We're having tea. Then Ethan and me are going to watch our film.'

'Again, sweetie? Doesn't Auntie Sarah want to watch something else on TV?' He chuckled as a woman's voice sounded, saying that if it kept the kids quiet, she was happy.

'Listen, Ellie...' He waited until the commotion on the other end of the line subsided. 'Ellie, Daddy's got to work, so you'll be staying with Auntie Sarah for tonight.'

Silence. Then a little voice sounded. 'I know. Miss you, Daddy.'

Cass almost choked with emotion. When she looked at Jack, he seemed to have something in his eye. 'I miss you too, sweetie. You know you're always my number one girl. And I'll be back soon to give you big hugs.'

'How big?'

'As big as a bear. No, bigger than that. As big as our house.'

A little squeal of delight from Ellie. Cass imagined that Jack's hugs were something to look forward to.

'As big as our house...'

'Yeah.' Jack was grinning broadly now. 'Be good for Auntie Sarah, won't you.'

'I'm always good.' Ellie's voice carried a note of reproof.

'Sure you are. Would you like to meet my new friend?' He winked at Cass and her heart jolted so hard she almost fainted. 'She's a firefighter.'

'She has a fire engine?' Ellie was obviously quite taken with the idea.

'Why don't you ask her?' Jack chuckled and handed the phone over to Cass.

A little girl was staring at her. Light brown curls and luminous brown eyes. She was the image of Jack.

'Hi, Ellie. I'm Cassandra.' She wondered whether Ellie was a bit young to get her tongue around the name. Child development wasn't her forte. 'All my friends call me Cass.'

'You're a fire lady? With a fire engine?' Ellie was wriggling excitedly.

'Yes, that's right.'

'Do you have a ladder?'

'Yes, more than one. And we have a hose, for putting out all the fires.'

'Auntie Sarah...!' Ellie clearly wanted to share this exciting news.

'Yes, I heard. Tell Cassandra that you've seen a fire engine.' The woman's voice again, laughing.

'I've seen a fire engine.' Ellie turned the edges of her mouth down theatrically. 'It was a long, long, long way away...'

Suddenly Cass knew exactly what to say to Ellie. 'Tell you what. We're having an Open Day at our fire station soon. We're showing all the children around...' She was about to add that Ellie would have to ask her father if she might come, but that seemed to be a foregone conclusion.

'Yesss! Daddeee!'

Jack shot Cass a wry smile. 'Do I get to come along too, Ellie?'

Cass thought she could almost see the little girl roll her eyes.

'You have to take me, Daddy. I can't drive...'

'Ah, yes, of course. Looks like it's the two of us, then. Say thank you to Cassandra.'

Jack leaned in, speaking over her shoulder, and Cass swallowed a gasp, suddenly aware that his body was very close.

'Thank you, Cassandra.'

Ellie managed the name without even blinking, and Jack chuckled.

'Time to say bye-bye now, sweetheart.' Ellie responded by waving and blowing a kiss, then Jack took the phone from her to say his own goodnight to his daughter.

Cass stood up, her limbs suddenly trembling. It was impossible to fall in love in so short a time and over the phone. And, if she was honest with herself, she hadn't fallen in love with Ellie's brown eyes but with Jack's. But he was a grown man. It was much easier to admit that his child was all she could see.

'She's gorgeous.' Cass had let him finish the call, looking away when he blew kisses to Ellie.

'Yeah.' His fingers lingered lovingly over the blank screen for a moment, as if he couldn't quite let go of the memory of his daughter's face, and then he handed the phone back. 'I didn't think she'd manage to pronounce *Cassandra*.'

The second time he said her name was just as disturbing as the first. Awakening thoughts of what it might feel like to have him whisper it.

'She must be growing up fast.'

'Seems too fast, sometimes.' He shrugged. 'She loves fire engines...'

'Yeah, me too. You didn't mind me asking her to the Open Day?'

'Mind...?' He laughed. 'Sounds like fun. Do I get to sit in the driver's seat?'

'No. Children only. Dads get to watch.'

# CHAPTER THREE

THEY'D EATEN IN the church hall, the dreaded Monday Club turning out to be a group of perfectly nice women who cooked good food in large quantities and didn't mind a laugh. The evening was spent at the vicarage with Lynette and Cass, who persuaded Martin to make up a fourth for board games. Then Jack made his apologies and retired to his sleeping quarters, shutting the door and lying down fully dressed on the camp bed.

Suddenly he felt very alone. Ellie would be tucked up in bed by now and although he knew that Sarah would have given her bedtime kisses on his behalf, he hadn't been there to give them himself. Mimi was probably exhausted and looking forward to a good night's sleep. Cass was...

He wasn't going to think about where Cass was. He had a child, and he had to protect her. Jack had made up his mind a long time ago that the best thing for Ellie was that he remained single.

He must have drifted off to sleep because the next thing he knew was a tingle behind his ear, and his eyes shot open involuntarily as he realised that someone was rubbing their finger gently on his skin. He blinked in the light that was flooding in through the doorway and saw Cass.

For one moment all he could think was that this was a delicious way to wake up, coaxed out of unconsciousness by a red-haired goddess. Then the urgency on her face snapped him back to reality.

'Her waters have broken. Jack...'

'Okay. I hear you.' Jack swung his legs from the bed and shook his head to bring himself to. He'd been hoping that this wouldn't happen. He had the training and the experience for it, and this certainly wasn't the most outlandish place that he and Mimi had delivered a baby before now. But without the possibility of any backup, and only the medical supplies that Rafe had sent, it was a heavy responsibility, which he had to bear alone.

This was no time to panic. Contrary to all his expectations, Cass was panicking enough for both of them at the moment.

Keeping his pace brisk but unhurried in an effort to slow Cass down a bit, he picked up his medical bags and made for the vicarage. As they reached the back door they passed Martin, who was hurrying in the other direction, a sleeping child in his arms.

'Go through, Jack. Just getting the kids out of the way.'

Jack nodded. Following Cass through the kitchen and up the stairs, he found Sue and another woman on either side of Lynette, supporting her as she paced slowly up and down.

'We'll take her into my bedroom.' Sue looked up at him. 'There's an en suite bathroom, and the mattress in here is wet.'

'Thanks.' First things first. Jack smiled at Lynette, wiping a tear from her face. 'How are you doing?'

'Um... Okay. I think.'

'Good. You want to walk a bit more?'

Lynette nodded.

'All right. I'm going to get the other room ready for you, and then we'll take it from there. Tonight's your night, eh?'

'Yes... Thanks.'

Cass took Sue's place at Lynette's side, and Sue led him

through to her own bedroom. Jack pulled the plastic under-sheet from his bag, silently thanking Rafe for thinking to pack it, and Sue set about stripping the bed.

When Cass supported Lynette through to the main bed-room, it seemed that everything was ready. She helped her sister sit down on the bed. 'Do you want your scented candles?'

'No!' Lynette's flailing hand found Jack's sweatshirt and held on tight. 'I want to keep a close eye on the guy with the pain relief...'

'I'm here.' Jack was calm and smiling. 'I'm going to wash my hands and I'll be right back, okay.'

'Yeah. Whatever.' Lynette frowned and closed her eyes.

*Get the candles anyway...* Jack mouthed the words to Cass and she hurried through to the other room to fetch Lynette's hospital bag.

When she got back, Sue waved her towards the bathroom door and Cass tapped on it tentatively. Jack was standing in front of the basin, his T-shirt and sweatshirt hung over the side of the bath, soaping his hands and arms. 'There's a clean T-shirt and some dressings in my medical bag. Will you get them, please?'

'Dressings? What's the matter?'

'Nothing. They're for me.' He grinned, turning round, and she saw the new bruises on his chest, the bright red gashes that ran across his sternum and upper arms.

Her sister was in labour. Now was a fine time to notice that his muscle definition was superb. Or to feel a tingle at the warmth of his smile. Cass swallowed hard.

'How did you do that...?' She pointed to the spot on her own arm to indicate the patch of red, broken skin on his. That had to hurt.

'It's just a friction burn. It's bleeding a little so best I cover it up.'

She nodded and went to fetch what he'd asked for. The dressings, along with a roll of tape and some scissors, were right at the top of the bag. Jack must have been thinking ahead.

'Okay, will you tape these on for me, please? Right around the edge so that there are no openings anywhere.'

Couldn't Sue do it? The temptation to run away and hide from his body almost made her ask. But her sister was out there having a baby, and Cass had already decided she'd do whatever it took.

He held the gauze in place and she taped around it for him. Trying not to notice the fresh smell of soap on skin. Trying not to think about how close he was, or how perfect.

'Thanks. That's great.' He nodded his approval and Cass stepped back, almost colliding with the linen basket. Then, thankfully, he pulled the T-shirt over his head.

'Ready?' His smile held all of the warmth that she could want for Lynette. Which happened to be a great deal more than Cass could deal with.

'Yes. I'm ready.' Cass had told herself that this was going to be the best night of her life. Being with Lynette all the way, seeing her nephew being born. Now, all she could feel was fear, for everything that could go wrong.

He was calm and quiet, soothing Lynette when the contractions eased and helping her concentrate and breathe when they came again. When Lynette became frightened and overwhelmed, he was there with reassurance and encouragement. When she wanted to change position, he let her lean on him. When she needed pain relief, he was there with the Entonox.

Lynette seemed almost serene when she wasn't crying in pain, switching from one to the other with astonishing rapidity.

'Is this right?' Cass mouthed the words to Jack.

Jack's gaze flipped to the portable monitors at Lynette's side. 'Yeah, we're okay.'

'It's so fast…' Cass had been preparing for a long haul, but it had barely been an hour since she'd woken him up and already he was telling Lynette that they were nearly there.

'That's a good thing. Lynette's fine and so is the baby.'

Ten minutes later, her nephew was born. Jack cleared his mouth, rubbing his chest gently. Everyone held their breath and then the little man began to cry. Lynette squeezed Cass's hand so tight that she thought she was going to break her fingers.

'Say hello to your mum…' Jack laid the baby on Lynette's chest and covered him over with a towel. The two women lay on the bed together, cradling the baby, in a daze of happiness.

Suddenly, it was all perfect. Martin had welcomed the newest member of the village to the world, and Sue went to make tea and toast. Jack managed everything perfectly, melting into the background, clearing up and making the medical checks that were needed, without intruding into their bubble.

Then the call came from Lynette's husband, saying he'd received the photo that Cass had sent and was ready and waiting for a video call. Lynette was left alone for a few minutes to talk to him and show him their new son.

Cass waited outside the door, a sudden heaviness settling on her. However close she and Lynette were, however much her sister had needed her, it wasn't her baby. It was Lynette and Steven's. Their joy. One that she would only ever feel second-hand.

This wasn't the time. There were too many special moments ahead for her to spoil with her own selfishness. And they came soon enough. The moment when Jack helped Lynette to encourage her son to feed, and he finally got the hang of what he was supposed to do. The moment when his eyelids flickered open and Cass stared for the first time into his pale blue eyes.

'Do you have a name for him yet?' Jack was busy re-packing his medical bag.

'We did have. But we've decided on something different.' Lynette smiled. 'We reckon Noah.'

'Very appropriate.' Jack chuckled.

'Is Jack a nickname for John?' She was beginning to tire now, and had lost the thread of what she was saying a couple of times already.

'Yep. Named after my grandfather. They used to call him Jack as well.'

'Noah John has a nice ring to it, don't you think?'

Jack turned. 'What does your husband think?'

'Steven suggested it. What you did tonight meant everything, to both of us, and we'd really like to have your name as his middle name. If you don't mind, that is.'

A broad grin spread over Jack's face. 'I'd be very honoured. Thank you.' He walked over to the bed, bending down to stroke the side of little Noah's face with his finger. The tiny baby opened his eyes, seeming to focus on Jack, although Cass knew that he couldn't really focus on anything just yet.

'Hey there, Noah.' Jack's voice was little more than a whisper. 'We guys have to stick together, you know. Especially since we share a name now. What do you say we let your mum get a bit of rest?'

'Will you and Cass look after him for me? I just want to close my eyes; I don't think I can sleep.'

'Of course.' Sue had prepared the Moses basket that she'd used for her children and Jack took Noah, setting him down in the cradle. But he immediately began to fret and Jack picked him up again, soothing him.

'Now what do we do?' Cass whispered the words at Jack.

Sue and Martin had quietly left at the first suggestion of sleep, and Lynette's eyes had already drooped closed. It seemed that they were quite literally left holding the baby.

Jack chuckled quietly, nodding towards the easy chair in the corner of the room. 'Sit down. Over there.'

'Me?' She was suddenly gripped with panic. 'You want *me* to hold him?'

'I've got things to do. And it's about time he got acquainted with his aunt.'

It was almost a bitter thought. Holding her sister's baby and not her own. But in the peace and quiet of the room, candles guttering in their holders and a bedside lamp casting a soft glow, it was easy to forget that. Cass plumped herself down in the chair, wondering what Jack was going to do next.

'Suppose I drop him?'

'You won't.' Jack seemed to be able to manage the baby in one arm while he picked up a pillow from the bed in the other hand, dropping it on to her lap. 'Here you are. That's right.'

The sudden closeness felt so good she wanted to cry out. Jack's scent, mingling with that of a baby. Instinctively her arms curled around Noah and she rocked him gently, holding him against her chest. He fretted for a moment and then fell into a deep sleep.

'I just want to wake him up. See his eyes again...' She looked up at Jack and, when he smiled, Cass realised that all the wonder she felt must be written clearly on her face.

'Yeah, I know. Let him sleep for a while; being born is a tiring business.'

Jack fetched a straight-backed chair from the kitchen and sat in the pool of light from the lamp, writing notes and keeping an eye on everyone. When Cass could tear her gaze from Noah, she watched Jack. Relaxed, smiling and unbearably handsome. She envied the shadows, which seemed to caress his face in recognition of a job well done.

When Noah woke and began to fuss a little, Lynette was immediately alert, reaching for her child. Jack delivered him to her and this time there were fewer grimaces and less messing around to get him to feed. Cass watched from the other side of the bed and, when he'd had enough and fallen back into sleep, she curled up with her sister on the bed, holding her hand until they both followed Noah's example and slept.

The morning dawned bright and clear. Jack had managed to sleep a little, in the chair in the corner of the room, and now he had heard from the HEMS team. They were flying, and would take advantage of the break in the weather to take Lynette and Noah to hospital.

Despite the early hour, a few people had gathered around the village green. An excited chatter accompanied the landing of the helicopter and a ragged cheer went up when its crew followed Jack towards the vicarage.

He said his goodbyes to Lynette and Noah inside, keeping his distance as the HEMS team took them outside with Cass. Jack wondered if this would be the last he ever saw of her and, despite all his resolutions, he found himself staring at her, as if to burn her image into his mind. But she waited for Lynette and the baby to be safely installed in the helicopter and then jogged back to stand at his side.

'There goes your last chance of getting out of the village today. The roads are still blocked.' Cass's eyes seemed to be fixed on the disappearing speck in the sky.

Jack nodded. 'Yours too.'

'What does that make us?' She turned her querying gaze on to his face.

Jack shrugged. 'It makes us people who know our families are safe, and that the village might still need us.'

'It's not easy…'

'I don't think it's meant to be.' Jack's decision to stay had been made in the small hours of last night and it had torn him in two. Doing his job and being a good dad was a complex and sometimes heartbreaking juggling act.

'Well, it's done now. The only thing I can do to justify it is to make today count.' She smiled suddenly. 'Hungry?'

'Famished.' He looked at his watch. 'What time's breakfast?'

'Not for a couple of hours. We'll raid the kitchen.'

The kitchen was empty and she made toast while Jack made the tea. She rummaged in the cupboard, finding a couple of jars, and picked up two bananas from a crate in the corner. Then she led the way through to her private hidey-hole in the church porch.

'What is that?' It appeared that instead of choosing what she wanted on her toast, Cass was going for everything.

'Chocolate spread, then peanut butter and mashed banana. Try it; it's really nice.'

'Maybe another time. When I'm planning on not eating for the next two days.'

'A good breakfast sets you up for the day. You should know that; you're a medic.'

'Yeah. Perhaps I'd better not mention the sugar in that.' She shrugged. 'I'll work it off.'

They ate in silence. His first slice of toast with peanut butter and his second with chocolate spread. Jack supposed that since he was going to eat the banana afterwards, he couldn't really poke too much fun at Cass's choice of breakfast.

It was still early and the glow of a new day, diffusing gently through the thick ancient glass, seemed to impose a relaxed camaraderie. Grabbing meals at odd hours after working most of the night. Talking, saying whatever came to mind without the usual filter of good manners and expediency. It felt as if anything could be asked, and answered.

'Is there someone waiting for you when we get out of here?'

She shrugged. 'Lots of people, I imagine.'

'I meant a partner...' It was becoming important to Jack to find out about all the subjects that Cass seemed to skirt around.

'Oh, that.' Jack wondered whether she really hadn't known what he was talking about. 'Big red truck. Makes a noise...'

'You're married to your job, then?'

She nodded, taking a bite from her toast. 'You?'

'I never married. And I don't get much time for socialising any more; when Ellie came along I had to make quite a few changes.'

She turned her querying eyes on to him and Jack wondered whether she wanted to know about him as much as he wanted to know about her. It was strangely gratifying.

'Then you have a *past*? How exciting.' The curve of her lip promoted an answering throb in his chest which made it hard to deny how much he liked it when Cass teased him.

'It's not that exciting.' Looking back, it seemed more desperate than anything. Desperate to find the warmth that was missing from his broken home, and yet afraid to commit to anyone in case they let him down, the way his father had let his mother down.

She gave him that cool once-over with her gaze which always left his nerve endings tingling. 'Bet you were good at it, though.'

That was undeniably a compliment, and Jack chuckled. 'I kept my head above water.'

Her eyes were full of questions, and suddenly Jack wanted to answer them all. 'Ellie's mother was the daughter of one of my dad's climbing partners; we practically grew up together. I went off to university and when I got back Sal was away climbing. It wasn't until years later that we found ourselves in the same place at the same time, for the weekend…'

'Okay. I've got your drift.' Cass held up her hand, clearly happy to forgo those particular details. 'So what about Ellie?'

'Fifteen months later, Sal turned up on my doorstep with her.'

'And you didn't know…?'

'Sal never said a word. She only got in touch then because she needed someone to take Ellie while she went climbing in Nepal.'

Cass choked on her toast. 'That must…I can't imagine what that must have been like.'

'It was love at first sight. And a wake-up call.'

'I can imagine. Bachelor about town one minute, in charge of a baby the next. However did you cope?'

'Badly at first. Sarah took me in hand, though; she got me organised and offered to take Ellie while I was at work.' Despite all of the sleepless nights, the worry, it had felt so right, as if he'd been looking for something in all the wrong places and finally found it on his own doorstep. He'd had no choice but to change his lifestyle, but Jack had done so gladly.

'And Ellie's mother?'

'She never came back. Sal died.'

Cass's shoulders shook as she was seized with another choking fit. Maybe he should wait with the story until she'd finished eating.

She put the toast down on to her plate and left it there. 'Jack…I'm so sorry. She was killed climbing?'

'No, she was trying to get in with an expedition to Everest. Of course no one would take her; there's a waiting list to get on to most of the peaks around there and you can't just turn up and climb. She wouldn't give up, though, and ended up sleeping rough. She was killed in a mugging that went wrong.'

'Poor Ellie...'

Her immediate concern for his child touched Jack. 'She's too young for it to really register yet. I just have to hope that I can be there for her when it does.'

Cass took a sip of her tea. 'I have a feeling you'll do a great job of helping Ellie to understand about her mother, when the time comes.'

'What makes you say that?'

She flushed pink. 'Because you're very reassuring. You were great with Lynette last night. In between all the grimaces, that was her *I'm very reassured* face.'

'Well, that's good to know. And what was yours?' He pulled a face, parodying wide-eyed panic.

Cass giggled. 'That was my *I hope no one notices I'm completely terrified* face.'

'Thought so.' He leaned towards her. 'I don't think anyone did.'

'That's okay, then.' The sudden glimpse behind the barriers that Cass put up between her and the world was electrifying. Her smiles, her laughter were bewitching. If things had been different...

But things weren't different. Ellie had already lost her mother. No one should feel that loss twice, and if it meant that Jack remained steadfastly single it was a small price to pay for knowing that no one would ever have the chance to leave Ellie again.

He took a gulp of tea. Maybe it was better to just stop thinking about any of this and focus on the here and now. 'So what are your plans for the day?'

Crisis bonding. That was what it was. Jack wouldn't seem half as handsome or a quarter as desirable if it hadn't been for the floods and a long night, filled with every kind of emotion imaginable. A little sleep and a lot of coffee would fix everything.

Somehow Cass doubted that. But she had to tell herself something before she started to fall for Jack. Because, when it came down to it, his expectations were most probably the same as any other man's.

And she would never really know what his expectations were until she was in too deep. When Paul had first proposed to her he'd never mentioned children, but the pressure had started to grow as soon as it became apparent to both of them that there might be a problem. She couldn't risk the pain of trying again and being rejected when she failed. No man, not even Jack, could guarantee that he wouldn't leave her if she couldn't give him children.

It was better to accept being alone. And to concentrate on today.

'Martin and I were going to go and visit Miss Palmer. She's eighty-two and won't leave her house. She's pretty feisty.'

He chuckled. 'What is it about this village? It's like a nineteen-fifties horror film—some poor hapless paramedic washed up to find himself in a remote place where all the women are terrifying...'

He wasn't terrified at all; he was man enough to enjoy it. Cass grinned. 'We *are* all terrifying. There's something in the water.'

Jack leaned back, his shoulders shaking with laughter. 'I'll stick to bottled, then. And I don't much like the sound of an eighty-two-year-old on her own in these conditions. Want me to come along?'

'Yes. Thanks. Maybe we can grab a couple of hours sleep first, though. And some coffee.'

# CHAPTER FOUR

'I WONDER IF she's got any cake.' Sleep seemed to have made Cass hungry again.

'Almost certainly.' Martin opened the front gate of one of a small, neat row of houses. 'I gather that the Monday Club came round here yesterday, after your visit.'

'That's all right then. What we can't eat, we can use to shore up the flood defences.' Cass stopped at the end of the path and Jack decided to wait with her, leaving Martin to approach the cottage alone.

The door was opened by a small, neatly dressed woman who might or might not be Miss Palmer. She didn't look eighty-two.

'Vicar. Lovely to see you.' She craned around to look at Cass and Jack. 'You've brought reinforcements, I see.'

Martin's shoulders drooped. Clearly, reinforcements were exactly what he needed.

'That her?' Jack murmured the words to Cass and she nodded, turning her back on the front door.

'Yep. She's...'

'Cassandra!' Cass jumped and swivelled back to face Miss Palmer. 'Do turn around, dear; you know I can't hear you.'

'Sorry. I forgot...'

Miss Palmer pursed her lips in disbelief. 'Well, come

in and have a cup of tea. And you can tell me all about last night.'

'News travels fast.' Cass strode up the front path. 'They're calling him Noah. Eight pounds, give or take.'

'Good.' Miss Palmer beamed her approval, leaning round to examine Jack. 'Is this your captive paramedic, dear?'

Jack was beginning to feel as if he was. Captivated by Cass's smile, longing to hear her laugh. Wanting to touch her.

'Yes. We found him washed up by the side of the river and we've decided to keep him. We've had him locked in the church hall.'

Miss Palmer nodded, enigmatic humour in her face. 'Leave your boots in the porch.'

The sitting room was bright and frighteningly clean, with the kind of orderliness that Jack remembered from before he'd had a child. One wall was entirely given over to glass-fronted bookcases and another was filled with framed photographs.

'My travels.' Miss Palmer caught Jack looking at them and came to stand by his side. 'Papua New Guinea... South Africa...'

Jack studied the black and white photographs. Some were the kind a tourist might take, posed with landmarks and things of interest, and others told a different story. Groups of children, ramshackle schools, a young woman whose air of determination couldn't be disguised by time and who had to be Miss Palmer.

'You worked abroad?'

'Yes. I'm a teacher. I came home when my mother became ill and looked after her for some years. Then I taught in the school, here.'

'And this one?' A colour photograph of Miss Palmer, done up in waterproofs and walking boots, standing on high ground. Next to her, Cass had her arms held aloft in an unmistakable salute to some victory or other.

'Ah, yes.' Miss Palmer shot Cass a smile. 'We climbed Snowdon.'

'Miss Palmer raised a whole chunk of money...' Cass added and Miss Palmer straightened a little with quiet pride.

'Surprising how much people will sponsor you for when you're in your seventies.' A slight inclination of the head, as if Miss Palmer was sharing a secret. 'They think you're not going to make it to the top.'

'We showed them, though.' Cass broke in again.

'Yes, dear. We did.' Jack found himself on the end of one of Miss Palmer's quizzical looks. She was probably checking that he understood the point that she'd just made. If she could do all this, then a flood wasn't driving her from her home.

'I'll go and make the tea. Make yourselves comfortable.' Martin sat down suddenly, as if responding to an order. Jack reckoned that any prolonged exposure to Miss Palmer would have that effect on someone.

'I'll come and give you a hand.' Jack ignored Cass's raised eyebrows, motioning for her to stay put. He wanted to speak with Miss Palmer on her own.

She bustled, tight lipped, around the small modern kitchen. Jack gave her some space, leaning in the doorway his arms folded.

'So. What are we going to do, then?'

Miss Palmer faced him with a look of controlled ferocity. Jack imagined that she was used to a whole class quailing into silence at that.

'I had assumed you might be off duty.' She glared at his T-shirt and sweater.

'I'm never off duty. I dare say you can understand that.' Miss Palmer didn't stop being a teacher as soon as she was out of the classroom. And Jack didn't stop being a paramedic just because his ambulance had been wrecked and his uniform soaked through.

'Yes, I do.' She laid cups and saucers carefully on a tray.

'Your friends are concerned about you. My job is to find out whether that concern is justified. To check whether you're okay, and if you are to leave you alone.'

Miss Palmer's set expression seemed to soften a little. 'This house is well above the flood line, and I'm lucky enough to have electricity and my phone still. Is it so much to ask, that I stay in my own home?'

'No. And I'll do my best to make sure that happens, but you've got to help me. If we can address any potential problems now, then that's a good first step.'

'Is this the way you deal with all the old ladies?'

'Yes, of course. Is this the way you deal with all your pupils?'

Miss Palmer smiled suddenly, her blue eyes twinkling with amusement. 'A hundred lines, young man. *I will not answer back.*'

Jack chuckled. He could see why Cass liked her so much; they were birds of a feather. Both as feisty as hell, with a sense of humour. 'Are you on any medication?'

Miss Palmer walked to the refrigerator and drew out a cardboard packet, which Jack recognised. 'Warfarin. What's that for—you have a blood clot?'

'A very small one. The doctors picked it up on a routine screening six months ago. I had an appointment for an X-ray a couple of days ago, to see whether the clot had dissolved yet, but I couldn't make it.'

'Okay. When was your last INR test?'

'Two weeks. I can't get to the hospital.'

'I'll get a test sent over; I can do one here.'

Miss Palmer nodded. 'Thank you. My INR is usually quite steady but...'

'Best to check.' The Warfarin would be thinning her

blood to dissolve the clot. The INR test made sure that the dose was correct. 'Do you have some way of calling someone? In an emergency?'

Miss Palmer opened a cupboard and reached inside, producing a panic alarm.

'Is that working?' First things first. Then he'd tell her that there wasn't much point in keeping it in the cupboard.

'Yes, I try it out once a week.'

'I want you to check it every evening. And I want you to wear it.'

He was expecting some kind of argument but Miss Palmer nodded, putting the red lanyard around her neck and tucking the alarm inside her cardigan.

'I want it within reach at all times. Particularly when you're in bed or in the bathroom.'

'You're very bossy, aren't you?' Miss Palmer seemed to respect that.

'Yeah, very. But I'll make you a deal. You wear the alarm and let me give you a basic medical check, and I'll get everyone off your back.'

Miss Palmer held out her hand and Jack smiled, stepping forward. Her handshake was unsurprisingly firm. 'All right. Deal.'

Jack had obviously been carrying out some negotiation in the kitchen. When he reappeared with Miss Palmer, carrying the full tray of tea things for her, it was apparent that they'd struck up some understanding. At least he'd got her to wear her alarm.

Tea was drunk and Martin excused himself, leaving to make a call on another family in the street. Cass concentrated on her second slice of cake while Jack busied himself, taking Miss Palmer's blood pressure, asking questions about her general health and checking on her heart and breathing.

Finally he seemed satisfied. 'Congratulations. I can find absolutely nothing wrong with you.'

'Not for want of looking.' Miss Palmer gave a small nod as Jack slipped the blood pressure cuff from her arm and she rolled down her sleeve. She liked people who were thorough in what they did, and clearly she approved of Jack.

'I'll be back with the INR test, and I expect to see you wearing your alarm.' Jack grinned at her. 'I might try and catch you by surprise.'

Miss Palmer beamed at him. 'Off with you, then.' She hardly gave him time to pack his bag before she was shooing him towards the door. Cass followed, hugging Miss Palmer and giving her a kiss on the cheek.

'Go carefully, Cassandra.'

'I will. You too, Izzy.' She whispered the name. It was something of an honour to call Isobel Palmer by her first name, reserved for just a few dear friends, and Cass didn't take it lightly.

She followed Jack down the front path and walked silently beside him until she was sure that Miss Palmer could no longer see them from her front window. 'All right, then. Give.'

He turned to her, raising an eyebrow. 'I've done a deal with her. She gets to stay as long as I'm allowed to satisfy myself that she's well and taking sensible precautions.'

'I don't like it.' Cass would much rather have her friend looked after for the time being. Martin had offered a place at the vicarage and, now that Lynette was gone, there was more than enough room.

'I know you don't. Look at it this way. What's important to her?'

'Her independence. I know that. But this wouldn't be for long.'

'That doesn't make any difference. Her community has

still told her, loud and clear, that she can't cope. How do you suppose that's going to affect her in the long term?'

He had a point. 'But… Look, I really care about her.'

'Yes, that's obvious. And if there were any medical reason for her to leave her home, I'd be the first to tell you. But I'm not going to provide you with an excuse to make her leave, because taking away an elderly person's independence isn't something that anyone should do lightly.'

Cass pressed her lips together. Izzy had helped her be independent when no one else could. Maybe it was fate that Jack was asking her to do the same for Izzy.

'Okay. You're right.' She pulled her phone out of her pocket and stuffed the earbuds into her ears. Before she got a chance to turn the music on, one of them flipped back out again as Jack nudged the cable with one finger.

'So what's the story with you and her? She was your teacher?'

'Yeah.'

'And you stayed in touch with her when she retired?'

He seemed to see almost everything. Which was obviously a good thing when it came to his patients, but Cass reckoned it could get annoying for everyone else.

'She was my teacher for twenty years. Still is, in some ways. I have dyslexia, and she took me on. I used to go to hers to do my homework after school every day and she used to help me.'

'And she let you struggle a bit with things?'

A grudging laugh of assent escaped her lips. 'She let me struggle all the time. She was always there to catch me, though.'

He nodded. 'Then perhaps that's your answer.' He picked up the earbud, which dangled on its lead against the front of her jacket, and gently put it back into her ear. Cass pretended not to notice the intimacy of it, but shivered just the same.

It appeared that even though the crisis was over, the bonding part wasn't. And wanting him, wanting Jack's strength and his warmth, would only end badly. She and Paul had tried for two years to have children, and by the end of it she'd been a wreck. Sex had become a chore instead of a pleasure and Cass had felt herself dying inside, unable to respond to a touch.

Worst of all, she'd become fearful. Afraid of a future that seemed to depend on her being able to have a child, and hardly daring to get out of bed on the mornings when her period was due. Fearful of the heartbreak that had come anyway, when Paul had left her.

That fear had paralysed her whenever she'd even thought about starting a new relationship, because any man would be sure to react in the same way as Paul had. So Cass had turned to the parts of her life where she'd already proved she could succeed. Her job. Taking care of her family and friends. Overcoming her dyslexia. If wanting Jack brought her loneliness into sharp focus then he would be gone soon, and the feeling would pass.

Cass had withdrawn into silence as they'd trudged back to the church hall. The weather was getting worse, rain drumming against the windows, and when Cass didn't show up for lunch Jack wondered if there was something wrong. It seemed almost as if the violence of the storm might be some response to the unspoken emotions of a goddess.

Nonsense. She might look like an ethereal being but she was all woman. Tough and proud on the outside but with a kernel of soft warmth that showed itself just briefly, from time to time. Each time he saw it, the urge to see it again became greater.

And that was nonsense too. His own childhood had been marred by loss and he wanted no more of it, not for himself or for Ellie. The uncertain reward didn't justify the risk, even if he did crave the sunshine of Cass's smile.

Cups and saucers were filled and the lines of diners started to break up into small groups, talking over their coffee. At the other end of the hall, Martin was on his feet, talking intently to a man who had hurried in, a small group forming around them. Someone walked out of the hall and Jack heard Cass's name being called.

Ripples of concern were spreading through the community, people looking up from their conversations and falling quiet. Jack stood up, walking across to Martin.

'What's going on?'

'Ah, Jack.' Martin's face was creased with anxiety. 'We've got a lost child...'

Activity from outside the hall caught Jack's attention. The shine of red hair through the obscure glass of the doors and then Cass was there, the man who had gone to fetch her still talking quickly to her, obviously apprising her of the situation.

'What do you want me to do?' Without noticing it, Jack seemed to have gravitated automatically to her side.

She looked up at him. The defeated droop of her shoulders that he'd seen earlier was gone; now Cass was back from whatever crisis she'd been facing. Full of energy and with a vengeance.

'We have a ten-year-old who's gone missing. We'll split up and search for him in teams. You're with me?'

Jack nodded. Of course he was with her.

# CHAPTER FIVE

JACK FOUND HIS jacket amongst the others, hung up on the rack in the lobby, and pulled his boots on. People were spilling out of the church hall, finding coats and forming into groups. Everyone seemed to know what they were doing and Cass was at the centre of it all.

Suddenly, she broke away from the people around her, walking over to a young woman in a wet jacket.

'We're going to find Ben now, Laura.' Cass put an arm around the woman's shoulders. 'Can you think of anywhere he might have gone?'

'He might be looking for Scruffy. He ran off and we couldn't find him. Pete went out this morning, but there was no sign of him back at the house.'

Cass nodded. 'Okay. And where might Ben be looking?'

'I don't know…' Laura shook her head and Cass took her gently by the shoulders.

'It's okay. Take your time.' She was calm and quite unmistakably in charge of the situation. Just what Laura needed at the moment.

Laura took a deep breath. 'Maybe… Oh, Cass. Maybe he's gone down to the river. We take Scruffy for walks along there.'

'Whereabouts? Down by my place?'

'Yes… Yes, that's right.'

'Okay, I'll check that out.'

'I'm coming…' Laura grabbed hold of Cass's jacket.

'I need you to stay here so that we can bring him straight back to you when we find him. Join the group that's searching the church buildings and keep your phone with you so I can call you. All right?'

Laura nodded. Jack knew that Cass was keeping her away from the river, and the reason didn't bear thinking about.

'Let go of me, then…' Cass gently loosened Laura's fingers from her jacket and turned, leaving her with Martin. Her face set suddenly in a mask of determination as she faced Jack.

'I'll get my bag…' The heavy bag would slow him up but he might need it.

'Thanks. If you give it to Chris, he'll stay here with the car. He can get whatever we need down to us quickly.'

'Okay. Makes sense.'

Jack fetched his bag and handed it over to a man standing by an SUV which was parked outside the church hall. Then he joined Cass's group and they set off, moving quickly through the village and down the hill.

They passed the spot where the bridge had been washed away yesterday, and Cass stopped to scan the water. 'I can't see anything…' She stiffened suddenly and pointed to a flash of blue and red in the branches of a partially submerged tree. The wind caught it and it flapped. Just a torn piece of plastic.

'Where *is* he?'

The exclamation was all she allowed herself in the way of emotion. After surveying the river carefully, she started to walk again. They scaled a rocky outcrop which afforded a view across the land beyond it.

Nothing. Jack strained his eyes to see some sign of the boy. The house ahead of them must be Cass's, stone-built and solid-looking, the extension at the back blending so well with the stonework at the front that it would be difficult to say for sure that it was modern if he didn't already know. He hoped that Ben hadn't got in there; the river had broken its banks and the place was surrounded by water.

'Ben...' Cass filled her lungs and shouted again. 'Ben!'

She stilled suddenly, holding her hand out for quiet. Nothing. Just the relentless sound of the rain. Then she suddenly grabbed Jack's arm. 'Can you see something? Down there?'

Jack squinted into the rain but all he could see was the swollen river, flanked on this side by twenty feet of muddy land. The river must have flooded up across it in the night and receded slightly this morning because he recognised part of the bridge sticking out of the quagmire.

She pulled a pair of binoculars from inside her coat and trained them down on to the mud. Then her breath caught. 'Got him. He's down by that bit of bridge. He's covered in mud and it looks as if he's up to his waist in it.' She lowered the binoculars, feeling in her pocket. Jack squinted at the place she'd indicated and thought he saw movement.

Cass handed a set of keys to one of the other men in the group. 'Joe, I've got a ladder in my garage and a couple of tarps. Can you guys go and find them, please?'

'Okay. Anything else?'

'Yeah, just pump out the water and clear up a bit while you're there.' A small twist of her lips and that wry joke was all she allowed herself in the way of regret.

She was off before Jack could say anything to her, scrambling down the other side of the ridge. The four men with them headed towards the house and Jack followed Cass, getting to the bottom before she did and catching her arm when she slipped in the mud.

'Careful...'

'Yeah, thanks.' One moment. There was no time to tell

her that he was sorry to see her house flooded, and no time for Cass to respond. But her brief smile told him that she knew and she'd deal with it later. Jack resolved to be there when she got around to doing that.

They set off, jogging towards Ben. Jack could see him now, covered in mud, sunk up to his waist, right next to the remains of the bridge. And, huddled next to him, wet through and perched on one of the stones, was a small black and white dog.

'He must have seen the dog and tried to get out there to fetch him.' Jack supposed that Scruffy was light enough to scamper across the mud, but the boy had sunk when he'd tried to follow him.

'Yeah. Wonder how close we can get.'

Jack had been wondering that himself. It was likely that the ground all around Ben was completely waterlogged.

'Ben... Ben...' Cass called over to the boy and Jack saw his head turn. 'Ben, stay still for me. I'm coming to get you.'

'Cass...' The boy's voice was full of the excitement of seeing the cavalry ride over the hill. Full of the panic that he must have felt when he'd started to sink into the mud and found he couldn't get out.

'Ben—' Cass came to a halt at the edge of the mud. 'Ben, I want you to look at me. No...don't try to move. Stay still.'

The boy was crying but he did what she told him. 'I... can't...'

'I know. Just hang on in there and I'll be out to get you in a minute. Then your mum gets the job of cleaning you up.'

Her grin said it all. She was trying to replace Ben's terror with the more mundane fear of a ticking off at getting himself so dirty. Cass was edging forward slowly, testing the ground in front of her before she put her weight on it. Jack followed, ready to grab her if she started to sink.

'You'll be able to tell your friends at school that you got rescued by the fire brigade.' She was grinning at Ben, talking to him as she tested the ground ahead of her and to either side, and the boy seemed to calm a bit.

Her foot sank into the mud in front of her, a good fifteen feet away from Ben, and he began to howl with terror. 'Okay. Okay, Ben. It's okay.'

She reached back and Jack clasped her arm. A brief smiling glance that seemed to sear through the urgency of the situation. 'Don't let me sink...'

'I've got you.'

Another tentative step in the clinging mud. Another and her boot sank as far as her ankle. Jack felt her fingers tighten around his and he reached forward, gripping her waist and pulling her back.

'I think that's as far as we'll get...' She looked around, pulling her phone from her pocket and dialling.

'Joe, I need the ladder now. And there's a toolbox in the garage—can you take a couple of doors off their hinges and bring them over...?'

She turned back to Ben. 'All right, Ben. Just waiting for my ladder. Then I'll be out to get you.' She was doing her best to turn this into an exciting adventure and, although it wasn't totally working, Ben was a lot calmer now.

Jack looked round and saw two men appear from Cass's garage, one on each end of an aluminium ladder. Wading through the water, they reached dry land and made for them as fast as the muddy terrain would allow.

'Here we go, Ben.' Cass was keeping up a stream of reassurance. 'They're on their way.'

As soon as the men reached them, she stretched the double length of the ladder across the muddy ground towards Ben. More than halfway. When it was extended fully, it would reach him easily.

'Thanks, Joe. Have you called the emergency services? She turned to one of the men who had brought the ladder.

'Yes. They'll do what they can. I called up to the church

and they're sending the medical bag down. Pete and Laura are coming too.'

'Great, thanks.'

Jack and the other two men helped Cass drag a couple of heavy branches over, putting them under the end of the ladder to try and stabilise it. Then she took a deep breath, turning her face up to him.

'Cover my back, eh?'

'You've got it.'

He tested the ground at their end of the ladder and put all his weight on it to steady it. Cass began to crawl along it, pushing the extension towards Ben.

'We're going back to help with the doors.' He heard Joe's voice behind him. 'The screws are all painted in, so they're not coming off that easily.'

'She's going to need some help out there. Use a crowbar if you have to.' Jack knew that Cass wouldn't hesitate to say the same.

'Right you are.' Joe turned, jogging back towards the house.

Ben gave a little cry of relief when the end of the ladder reached him, grabbing it and wrapping his arms around it. There was a click as Cass locked the extension in place, and then she began crawling along the extension.

Jack applied all his weight to his end of the ladder. The other end seemed to be sinking a little, but not so much that it stopped Cass from reaching Ben. He wondered whether the boy saw the same as he had, when he'd been tangled in that tree yesterday and he'd opened his eyes and seen her there.

From the way that Ben grabbed at her, he did. He heard Cass laugh and saw her wrap one arm around the boy, trying to loosen the mud around his waist with the other hand.

'I don't think…' She called back without turning her head, 'I'm going to need a hand with this.'

It was as Jack had expected. 'They're coming with the doors now. I'll be out in a minute.'

'That'll be lovely. Thanks.' Her tone was much the same as if she was accepting a cup of tea, and Jack smiled. She was unstoppable. And quite magnificent.

As soon as the ladder had reached Ben, Scruffy had bolted from his perch, running across her back and over the mud to get to dry land. Cass kept her attention equally divided between not falling off the ladder and keeping Ben quiet and stopping him from trying to move. She could hear signs of activity behind her, along with general instructions from Jack about tarps and doors. Then his voice, calling over to her.

'I'm moving off the ladder now. Watch out.'

She braced herself as the ladder moved slightly, sinking another inch into the mud. Then, as someone else applied their weight to the end of it, it steadied again. Above her head, she heard the beat of a helicopter.

'Are they going to pull us out?' Ben was shivering in her arms, his head nestled against her shoulder.

'No, they can't do that.' Trying to drop a line and pull Ben out might tear him in half. 'They're probably just flying over to see what the situation is and how they can help us.'

'And then the fire engine...?'

'Yeah. Then the fire engine.' If Ben hadn't realised that there wasn't a way for a fire engine to get to them, she wasn't going to disillusion him. 'But they won't have anything to do because we'll have you out before they get here.'

'Okay.' Ben sounded almost disappointed.

'Ben...?' Face down in the mud, Cass couldn't see what was happening behind her, but she recognised Laura's voice.

'Mum!' Ben's high-pitched shriek was directed straight into her ear.

'Ben, I want you to do exactly what Cass tells you. Do you hear me, darling?'

Good. Someone must be with Laura, calming her and telling her what to say. Jack, perhaps. Only she was rather hoping that Jack might be on his way towards her.

'Yes, Mum.'

'Tell your mum that you're all right. That you'll be out soon.' Cass grinned at Ben. It would do him good to say it, and do Laura good to hear it.

'Will I?'

''Course you will.'

Ben called out the words, this time managing to direct most of the volume away from Cass and towards his mother. Then someone tapped her ankle gently.

'Can I join you…?'

Jack's voice behind her.

'Feel free.' She squinted round as her kitchen door slid across the muddy ground towards her.

The door moved, and sank a little into the mud as it took his weight, and then he was there beside her. The relief was almost palpable.

'Hey, Ben.' He was lying on his stomach on the door, grinning broadly. 'How are you doing?'

'Okay, thanks.' Ben puffed out a breath. 'Are *you* going to pull me out?'

# CHAPTER SIX

UNFORTUNATELY, PULLING BEN out wasn't an option. Mud rescue was difficult and physically demanding at the best of times, and this wasn't the best of times. The continuing rain meant that every time they moved some of the mud from around Ben's body, mud and water trickled back into the hole.

Working together, they found a solution. Jack reached down, scooping the mud up, while Cass shoved it as far from Ben as she could. As they worked, she became bolder, no longer shy of Jack's body. Using his strength to lever her own against, bracing her legs across his.

It was exhausting work. Ben was beginning to get really cold now and started to cry again, and Jack talked to him, encouraging him. Or was it Cass that he encouraged? She hardly knew, just that the sound of his voice kept her going, despite the growing ache in her arms.

'What do you reckon?' His eyes seemed almost brighter, warmer, now that the rest of him was almost entirely covered in mud.

'Yeah. Let's try it.'

'Okay. Be ready to take him.' Jack wrapped his arms around Ben. Gently, carefully, he began to lift him. Ben's feet came out of his wellingtons, leaving them stuck in the muddy pit, and Jack hoisted him clear.

A tremulous, excited babble of voices sounded behind them. Cass had almost forgotten that anyone else was here.

'Got him…?' Jack passed Ben over to her and the boy grabbed her, whimpering with cold and exhaustion.

'Yeah.'

'Okay, you shift over on to the door and I'll pull you both back.' Jack manoeuvred around her, working his way carefully back, and Cass felt him grip her ankles, pulling her back after him.

Her limbs were shaking with fatigue and Cass didn't know where Jack found the strength to drag her those few short feet. But he did, taking Ben out of her arms as soon as they were back on the grass and carrying him over to the SUV that was waiting to take them the short distance to the village. Laura and Pete followed, desperate to hold their son.

A hand gripped hers, hauling her to her feet. People clustered around her, patting her on the back and enquiring whether she was okay. Cass nodded shakily and, as she made for the car, a path opened up in front of her, everyone stumbling backwards to get out of the way.

Ben was in his mother's arms on the back seat of the car, Scruffy sitting close to him. The boy was wet, cold, very muddy, but seemingly otherwise unscathed. Jack gave Cass a nod in answer to her silent question. He was okay.

'We'll get him back now…' He signalled to the driver and got into the car next to Ben, Laura and the little dog. Pete pushed Cass into the front seat.

'Don't you want to go?'

'I'll see you up there…' Pete's eyes were glistening with tears. 'Go and get yourself dry.'

They drove to the vicarage and Martin ushered Jack upstairs, Ben in his arms. Laura followed and Sue propelled Cass into the kitchen.

'I'd hug you if you weren't so filthy…' Sue stripped off

her jacket and sweatshirt, nodding when she found that the T-shirt underneath was dry. 'Sit.'

Cass sat down, half in a dream. Sue's businesslike ministrations were just what she needed. She didn't need Jack to help her out of her overtrousers; he had other things to do. But a part of her wished that he didn't and that after the struggle that they'd shared so intimately they could have just a little time together.

'Feet wet...?' Sue loosened the laces of one of her boots, sliding two fingers inside as if she were a child. 'They feel all right. Drink this...'

Hot soup. Fabulous. 'Thanks, Sue.'

She sipped the soup, letting the warmth of the kitchen seep back into her bones. Then she laid her head on her hands. Just for a moment. She was so tired.

'Sorry about all the mess, Sue.' It seemed that Jack's voice alone, amongst all the other comings and goings in the kitchen, had the power to pull her back to consciousness. Cass looked up and saw him standing in the doorway. He'd taken off his muddy jacket and sweatshirt and his arms and face had been washed clean, presumably as a preliminary to examining Ben. His short hair glistened with a few stray drops of moisture.

'Nonsense.' Sue glared at him. 'How's Ben?'

'We've cleaned him up and I examined him. He's pretty tired now, and he had a nasty fright. But, physically, I can't find anything wrong with him.'

'Good. Anything I should do?'

'Plenty of liquids, something to eat. Keep him warm. Old-fashioned care.'

Sue smirked. 'I can do that. You two go and get cleaned up.'

Cass got to her feet and walked over to the sink. She'd

got mud on the table where she'd laid her head down. Sue whipped the wash cloth out of her hand.

'Leave that to me. Go.'

'No, it's okay…' Cass's protests were silenced by one slight incline of Jack's head. She was going with him.

He led her to the bathroom in the church hall, accepting towels from one of the Monday Club ladies who bustled in out of nowhere and left just as energetically. Putting them down on to the chair by the washbasins, he dumped a plastic bag he'd been carrying on top and then walked over to the door, flipping the lock.

'Boots.' His grin was warm, and far too tender to resist. Cass hung on to the washbasin while he unlaced her boots, pulling them off.

'What's this?' He'd tipped her face up to his, running his thumb across the sore spot in her hairline.

'Just a scrape. Is it bleeding?'

'Not all that much. I'll clean it up in a minute.' He searched in the plastic bag and produced a bottle of shampoo, which Cass recognised as her own, one of the toiletries that she must have left at Sue and Martin's. She reached for the bottle and he pulled it away.

'Let me do it.'

There was no desire in his face, no trace of wanting. Just the warmth of two comrades who finally had the opportunity to see to each other's needs instead of those of everyone else.

This would be okay. And she so wanted it. Someone to take care of her after a long night and an even longer day. There would be no complications, no threat of what might happen tomorrow, because Jack wouldn't be here tomorrow.

He pulled a chair over to the washbasin at the end of the row, which was equipped with a sprinkler tap. Testing the temperature of the water, he told her to close her eyes.

Cass felt herself start to relax. He was good at this, guiding the water away from her face, rubbing gently to get all of the mud out of her hair. Massaging the shampoo through, his firm touch sending tingles radiating across her scalp. His leg pressed against her side as he leaned over her.

Maybe there was just a bit of sensuality about this. Along with all the nurturing and the warmth—the things that she reckoned it was okay to take from Jack. Cass dismissed the thought. It was what it was and she was too tired, too much in need to question it.

Then the warm water running over her head and finally a rub with a towel. Cass opened her eyes, sitting up straight.

'Better now?'

'Much. Thank you.' She rubbed at her hair and he handed her a comb. She winced as the teeth passed over the abraded skin at her temple.

'Let's have a look at that.' He didn't wait for her to either agree or disagree, just did it. Gentle fingers probed and then he reached for the plastic bag again. 'I think you'll live. I'll put some antiseptic on it, though.'

The antiseptic stung for a moment but even that was refreshing. Jack had a lightness of touch that set her nerve endings quivering, but that would have to remain her little secret.

'Do something for me?' He raised one eyebrow and she smiled.

'What do you want?'

A slight twitch at the corner of his mouth. Then he sat down opposite her and carefully removed a haphazardly applied piece of plaster from his arm. Underneath, the skin was red raw, a fragment of wood protruding. Cass caught her breath. He must have ignored the injury, the splinter driving deeper into his skin as he'd worked, and it was going to hurt to get it out now.

'Do you have a pair of tweezers?'

He leaned over, producing a pair from the bag, but when

Cass reached for them he closed his hand over them, holding it against his chest. 'Gently does it, eh? I know you lot.'

'My lot?' Cass grinned. 'What's that supposed to mean? I'll have you know I'm medically trained.' All firefighters were.

'It's supposed to mean that you don't have to throw me over your shoulder and carry me out of here first. Then tip me in a heap on the ground and start pumping on my chest.'

'Think I couldn't? I have a technique, you know.' The truth was that she could just about manage it. He'd have much less trouble lifting her.

He was shaking his head, laughing. 'That's exactly what I'm worried about.'

He handed her the tweezers and pushed the bottle of antiseptic towards her. Cass positioned his arm on the vanity top and bent over it, looking carefully. He made no sound but the muscles in his arm twitched when she laid her finger close to the wound.

'You really should have a local anaesthetic for this.'

'Nah. Better to just get it over with. I've only got the strong stuff in the medical bag.'

And he was saving that in case someone else needed it. Cass gripped his wrist tight to steady his arm and drew out the first piece of the splinter. She was going to have to fish a little for the second piece, which had been driven deep into his arm.

She so hated hurting him but he was trusting her to have the nerve to do it. Trusting that her hand wouldn't shake and make things a whole lot worse. She steadied herself and pressed the tweezers into the raw skin, trying not to hear his sudden intake of breath.

'Sorry…' She had nothing to make the pain any better and Cass fought the urge to dip her head and kiss it away.

'That's okay. Got it all?'

Cass carefully examined the wound. 'Yes, I think so. Can't see anything else.'

'Antiseptic, then.'

She applied a generous measure, making sure that the wound was disinfected. 'Are your tetanus shots up to date?'

'Yes.'

'Then we're nearly done.' Cass leaned forward, stripping off his T-shirt, and Jack chuckled.

'What now? Is this all part of the technique too?'

'Just making sure there's nothing else you haven't told me about.'

She would have preferred to touch instead of just looking, but that would be a step too far. Cass found herself ignoring the scrapes and bruises and concentrating on the smooth contours of his shoulders and chest. Very nice. And, what was nicer still, he had the confidence to just sit there and meet her gaze without sucking in his stomach or trying to flex his shoulders. He was perfect, just as he was.

'Finished?' He raised an eyebrow.

'Yeah. I think you'll do. Do you want me to dress your arm?'

'We'll clean up first.' He gave her a bone-melting grin and stood up, picking his T-shirt up and throwing it over one shoulder. 'Stay there.'

He picked up the bag and disappeared around the corner, towards the showers. Then the sound of gushing water came from the only cubicle that contained a bath. He wouldn't. Would he? If he did, then she just might. Even thinking about it was sending shivers through her tired limbs.

'Come on.' He was back again, catching up two of the largest towels in one hand, and Cass followed him. When he opened the door of the cubicle a gorgeous smell hit her. Bath oil foamed in the steaming tub and there were candles propped on the window ledge and the vanity unit.

'You're not going to fall asleep in here, are you?'

She wondered what he'd say if she asked him to stick around and make sure. But he'd put one of the towels down on the rack and now he was halfway out of the door. It seemed he had no intention of staying.

'No. Just keep talking.'

'Right you are.' He closed the door behind him and Cass heard the sound of the shower in the next door enclosure.

She turned her back on the partition wall between her and Jack before pulling her sweater off and unbuttoning her shirt. As she slipped off her jeans, she caught herself instinctively glancing behind her as if his gaze, or perhaps her own fantasies, had the power to dissolve the partition while she wasn't looking.

When she stepped into the steaming water, sinking beneath the bubbles, she felt the warmth seep into her bones. Cass lay back, rubbing the ache out of her shoulders. Bliss. This was pure bliss.

Okay, so he'd been tempted. Jack would admit to that. But it was worth needing to apply a little self-control to have seen her face when she'd walked into the cubicle. When he'd found her slumped at the kitchen table, he'd known this was exactly what she needed.

'Still awake?' he called to her as the hot water drummed on to his shoulders, making the various scrapes he'd picked up over the last couple of days smart a little.

'Yes. You?' Cass's voice was clear, drifting through the gap between the top of the partition and the ceiling.

'Yeah, I'm awake.' Wide awake and trying not to think thoughts that he shouldn't. 'I'm sorry about your house.' He'd been meaning to say it for a while now, but Jack wasn't sure how to do it without hugging her. The partition between them rendered that now unlikely.

The sound of her moving in the water. 'It's okay. There are more important things.'

Yes, there were, and what had happened with Ben had underlined it. But that didn't mean that the loss of her house was nothing. Jack wondered when it was going to hit Cass, and renewed his promise to himself that he'd be there when it did.

'Thanks for the candles.' Her mind seemed to have drifted somewhere else. 'They're a nice touch.'

Jack couldn't stop himself from smiling. There was so little he could do for her. 'Wish I could have done more.'

'Cherubs? Or perhaps a few perfumed clouds hovering about…?' She laughed quietly.

'Both. Every cherub needs a cloud.'

'Ah. And a glass of champagne.'

'Why stop at a glass?' Jack smiled as he soaped himself, feeling the tension ebb from his shoulders. 'Want some caviar with it?'

'No. I'll take a burger. Home-made, with extra cheese. And chips. Plenty of salt and vinegar.'

'Of course you will. Anything else?' What would he do if she said the one thing he wanted to hear? It was a nice fantasy, but in reality he'd probably pretend he'd got soap in his ears and was temporarily deaf.

'Mmm. I'd normally say a mud mask, but actually I think I've had enough mud for one day. Someone to get the knots out of my shoulders.'

Jack didn't comment on that, for fear of sounding too interested in the position. 'And…?'

'A manicure. After I've had the burger, of course. What about you?'

Jack chuckled. 'Three or four handmaidens. One to hand me my towel and one to hold my champagne for me.'

'That's two spare. Send them in here, will you, I'll be needing some help with the after-bath beauty thing. And the swirling silken robes, of course.'

'Yeah. Naturally.' He stepped out of the shower and

switched off the water, dabbing at the abrasions on his chest and arms. 'What about the musicians?'

'Nah. Tell them to wait outside; it's getting a bit crowded in here.'

Jack pulled on the clean clothes that Martin had found for him and unlocked the cubicle door. The image of Cleopatra, rising from her bath and being dressed in silks and jewels, was doing nothing for him. Cass, wrapped in a towel, tired from the effort of saving a young boy's life, was far more entrancing.

When he heard her get out of the bath and pad over to the row of lockers by the showers, Jack kept his eyes, if not his mind, on the task of clearing away the shampoo and wiping the basin. A pause and then she appeared. Pink-cheeked and dressed in sweatpants and a sleeveless T-shirt, a hooded sweat top slung over her shoulder.

'I…thanks. For the bath.' It seemed that fantasy was only permissible when they weren't actually looking each other in the eye.

'My pleasure.'

She shrugged awkwardly. 'I might go and lie down now. Close my eyes.'

Her hand was on the door handle before he remembered what it was he'd been meaning to say to her. 'Hey, Cass. Wait.'

'Yes?'

'Do you think we made today count? Enough to justify staying behind?'

She smiled suddenly. 'Yes. We did.'

# CHAPTER SEVEN

CASS HAD BEEN opening out her camp bed when Sue intercepted her. Jack had apparently just happened to walk over to the vicarage and mention that Cass was going for a lie down and Sue had a comfortable, warm nest all prepared for her on the sofa in her kitchen. Far nicer than a rickety camp bed in one of the chilly communal rooms behind the church hall.

Warm and relaxed from her bath, she fell asleep until Sue woke her for an evening meal. It seemed that Jack wasn't joining them and after waiting in the vicarage kitchen for two hours, not daring to betray her interest in him by asking Sue where he was, she went back to sleep on the sofa.

She woke early the following morning. Everyone in the house was still asleep and she donned her jacket and boots and crept out of the back door and to the kitchen in the church hall.

'Sleep well?' A voice behind her interrupted her thoughts and Cass jumped guiltily, sending a teacup rolling across the worktop. It seemed that even thinking about Jack could summon him up out of nowhere.

'Yes, thanks. What are you doing up?'

'One of the guys on weather watch last night... Andy, I think...he woke me up early. Apparently the water levels have gone down overnight, and you've got a couple of escape routes already planned. He said the one down by the motorway…'

So that was the reason for his early start, and the fact he was wearing his ambulance uniform. He couldn't wait to get home. The only thing that was unexpected about that was the feeling of disappointment which tore at Cass.

'Yeah. We reckoned that was most likely going to be the easiest. We've got a boat down there, and my car's parked on the other side, so I'll give you a lift. I need to go and get some supplies.'

'Actually, I was wondering if you'd do me a favour.'

'Of course.' Anything.

'Martin and I made a few visits last night. There are a couple of people running low on repeat prescriptions, and there's a man who is overdue for a pacemaker check. And there's the INR test for Miss Palmer. I'll speak to the hospital; they should be able to make the testing equipment available to me for the day, so I can do it here.'

'You're…' The only piece of information that her mind seemed to comprehend was that Jack was coming back.

'It'll take me most of the day to get across to the hospital and collect what I need, do the tests and then take everything back again. I was wondering if you might help with that, so I get a chance to see Ellie.' His eyes were clouded. Jack obviously didn't much like asking for favours. But he needed this one.

'Of course I will. You go straight home and I'll go to the hospital, collect what you need and get the prescriptions. I can pick you up again when I'm done.' She held out her hand. 'You have a list?'

He hesitated, his hand wandering to his pocket. 'That's really good of you. Are you sure it's okay?'

'Stop arguing and give me the list. Go see your daughter.'

\* \* \*

They'd been piloted across the stretch of water which blocked the A389 by one of the men from the village, drowsy and complaining in the early morning light. Then the dinghy turned around, leaving them standing alone.

'What now?' Jack looked around for any clues as to what he was supposed to do next.

'We walk.' Cass shouldered her backpack and set off, not waiting for his reply. 'It's only a little way. I have my SUV parked in the driveway of that house up ahead.'

Jack followed her pointing finger. 'That's yours? The one camouflaged by mud?'

'Hey! I'll have you know that my car has the engine of a...' she flung her hands up, searching for a suitable description '...a cheetah.'

'A cheetah? What's that—likely to eat you if you get too close?' Jack teased her.

'No! The bodywork's a bit splashed, from when I drove it out of the village when the motorway started to flood.' She grinned up at him. 'You want to walk?'

'I'll take my chances.' Jack upped the pace a little and she matched his stride. The day ahead of them seemed suddenly full of promise.

She'd delivered Jack to a large, neatly groomed house on the edge of one of the villages, close to town. He'd left her with one of his delicious smiles to think about before jogging up the front path and ringing the doorbell. Cass thought about waiting to see whether Ellie would come to the door, and decided not to. She had other things to do and her own list, along with Jack's, would take a good few hours.

It took less than that, but she'd promised Jack that she'd pick him up at twelve and being early would only deprive him of precious time with his daughter. Cass stopped outside a coffee shop and found a seat at one of the smaller tables to drink her coffee alone.

At five past twelve she drew up outside the house again. Grabbing the bag on the front seat, she wondered for the fiftieth time whether this wasn't going to make her look an idiot.

'Sarah...?' A dark-haired young woman answered the front door. 'I'm Cass.'

'Come in.' Sarah shot her a broad smile that reminded her of Jack's. 'They're through here.'

She followed Sarah through to a large lounge. One end of it was strewn with toys and Jack was sitting at the other end in an armchair, a little girl on his lap, a child's picture book laid aside on the arm of the chair.

Two pairs of brown eyes. One shy and assessing, the other smiling.

'You got everything?'

'Yeah.'

Ellie's small fist was wound tight into her father's shirt and she was hiding her face now. Cass stood her ground, wondering what to do.

'Say hello to Cassandra, Ellie...' Jack nudged his daughter's arm, speaking quietly, and the little girl shot her a brief glance. 'She's a bit shy.'

'That's okay. I...er...I went for a coffee and happened to see this as I was walking back to the car. For Ellie...'

She proffered the package awkwardly. It was a mass of brown paper and sticky tape, probably not particularly attractive to a child. And Cass wasn't sure now whether the contents would be all that appealing either. Ellie looked like a very girly girl, in her little pink and blue dress and pink cardigan.

Jack rose from the chair, taking Ellie with him. The little girl clung to her father, hiding her face in his shoulder. 'Hey, Ellie. Cass has brought you something.'

Ellie turned, looking at her solemnly. Then suddenly she smiled.

'Hi, Ellie.' Cass smiled back.

'Hi, Cassandra.' Jack chuckled as Ellie once again managed to pronounce Cass's full name.

'Maybe Cassandra likes to be called Cass?' He raised one eyebrow and his daughter looked up at him.

'I like Cassandra,' the little girl corrected him firmly.

'Well, it's not a matter of what we like. We should call Cass whatever she likes to be called, shouldn't we?'

Ellie turned questioning eyes on to Cass.

'I like Cassandra too. It's just that most people call me Cass because it's shorter. But I'd like *you* to call me Cassandra.'

'See...' Ellie gave Jack an *I-told-you-so* look.

'Yeah, okay. Far be it from me to interfere...' He shot her a delicious grin. That hard, strong body, the tender eyes. The tough, unbending resolve that was all too easy for the little girl in his arms to conquer. It was like an arrow, straight to Cass's heart.

Ellie was reaching now for the parcel in her hand, and Cass handed it over. Jack peered at it. 'What d'you have there, Ellie?'

'I don't know...'

'Well, say thank you to Cassandra and then you can unwrap it.' Jack looked at the sticky tape. 'Maybe you can ask her to help you.'

He let Ellie down and she ran to the chair, putting the parcel on to the seat and pulling at the wrappings. Jack shrugged. 'Or she'll just try it herself...' He smiled at Cass. 'Thank you.'

'You're welcome. I just happened to see it and...'

'Cassandra!' Ellie had torn most of the brown paper off and scattered it on the floor, but the sticky tape was too much for her. Cass grinned, walking over to her and kneeling down next to her, tearing at some of the tape.

'Wow! Look at that, Ellie.' Jack's voice behind her. Ellie gifted her with a bright smile and suddenly everything was right with the world. 'Say thank you, and go and show Ethan and Auntie Sarah what you've got.'

'Thank you, Cassandra…' Ellie threw the words over her shoulder as she ran to the kitchen, where Sarah was making the tea.

'Every girl needs a fire engine?' When Jack turned, the curve of his lips was all for her. Not the indulgent smile that he had for Ellie, but something raw, male. The trace of a challenge, mixed with the promise of something heady and exciting, should she wish to take him up on it.

'I think so.' She was caught in his gaze, unable to back off.

'You're probably right.' He reached forward, brushing a strand of hair from her brow. 'Take your coat off. Sarah's making lunch and she won't let you go without something to eat.'

Sarah and Cass were a perfect foil for each other. Sarah loved to cook, and generally did so as if she were feeding an army, and Cass was perfectly capable of eating like one.

Ellie was allowed down from the table and disappeared off into a corner, clutching her fire engine and a red colouring crayon. Cass leaned back in her chair, her plate empty.

'Thank you. Your spaghetti sauce is really tasty.'

Sarah smiled brightly. 'Would you like the recipe?'

'If you don't mind. I'd like to have a go at this myself.'

Somehow Jack hadn't imagined Cass doing anything as mundane as exchanging recipes. Charging to the rescue seemed more her style. Or maybe testing her strength against his at midnight, under a starry sky. But, when he thought about it, the idea of coming home to find her cooking was equally intoxicating.

'You cook?' He smiled, as if the question were a mere pleasantry.

'I like to eat.' She grinned back. 'That generally involves cooking first.'

'I'll email it through to you. Text me your email address.' Sarah collected the plates and turned to the refrigerator. 'Anyone for cheesecake?'

Cass's grin indicated that she was more than a match for cheesecake.

Ellie had presented her with a picture. A large figure, which seemed to be her, from the amount of red crayon that had been applied around the head, towering over a red box on wheels. Cass hugged the little girl, genuinely delighted, and felt Ellie plant a kiss on her cheek.

Jack had pencilled in her name under the figure and Ellie had returned to her corner to laboriously trace out the letters, her tongue stuck out in concentration. Then it was time to leave. Cass bade Sarah and Ellie goodbye and waited in the car while Jack hugged his daughter.

He dodged out, rain spattering his jacket, and Cass whipped Ellie's picture off the front passenger seat before he sat on it.

'Not a bad likeness.' He smiled at her.

'She's even put a ladder in.' Cass indicated the miniature ladder that the giant figure was brandishing.

'Yep. She's got an eye for detail, even if she's a bit wobbly on scale still.' He regarded the picture thoughtfully. 'And your hair…'

'Yeah. Rub it in.' Sometimes Cass wondered whether her hair was all people saw about her. The phrase *flame-haired firefighter* had worn thin a while ago.

He gave her a reproachful look. 'I was going to say that

Ellie did her best with the colours she had. It would be a bit much to ask for her to do it justice.'

The look in his eye told Cass that this was a compliment. The thought that Jack liked her hair suddenly made all the jokes about it worthwhile.

'Would you mind if we stopped off at my place? I want to get a change of clothes…'

Cass caught her breath. Maybe the change of clothes was just for today. Maybe he wasn't thinking about staying. She didn't dare ask.

'Yes, if you want.'

'That's if I still have a bed for tonight, in the church hall.'

'Of course you do. Thanks.'

'And if we could stop at the phone shop as well—it's on our way, and hopefully I'll have a replacement phone waiting for me.' He grinned. 'I called them this morning and asked, told them it was an emergency and that I'm a paramedic. The woman on the other end was really helpful.'

The grey, clouded sky suddenly seemed warmer, less forbidding. Cass started the engine, craning around to see over the boxes stacked in the back of the SUV, and reversed out of Sarah's drive.

Jack's house was only ten minutes away. He motioned for her to follow him inside and left her in the sitting room while he disappeared upstairs.

The room had a nice feel to it. A little battered in places, which was clearly the result of a four-year-old's exuberance, and the toys in the corner were stacked anyhow, as if they'd been hurriedly cleared away before Jack left for a day's work. But it was comfortable. The way a home should be. A sudden vision of her own ruined home floated in front of her eyes and Cass blinked it away.

The open fireplace was obviously used, coal heaped in a scuttle beside it. The dark leather sofa was squashy and comfortable, piled with cushions, a couple of throws across the back rest. Bookshelves, on either side of the chimney piece, were stacked full, the bottom shelf clearly reserved for Ellie, as it contained children's picture books. The very top shelf boasted a set of leather-bound books and Cass squinted up at the gold leaf titles on their spines. She couldn't read all of them, the words that were faded and cracked were a bit too much for her, but it was obviously a set of Victorian classics.

Some framed photographs obscured the backs of the books on the lower shelves. Pictures of Ellie, growing up. Jack, with Ellie on his shoulders. A woman, sitting on an elephant, her bright blonde hair obviously owing more to a bottle of peroxide than nature. It was impossible to tell whether Ellie's mother was like her at all; her face was twisted into an open-mouthed expression of exhilaration.

Another shot, obviously taken at a beach bar, and next to that one taken on the top of a snow-covered peak.

'The Matterhorn.' Jack came into the room.

'Looks fantastic.'

'Yeah. It's a popular peak.' When she turned, Jack's eyes were fixed on the photograph and she felt a stab of jealousy for Sal. Not because of all the places she'd been, the things she'd done, but because she was the woman who'd made love with Jack and borne his child. And that was wrong, on so many levels, not least because Cass had decided that she was not going to feel anything for Jack.

'You must miss her.'

Jack shrugged. 'These photos are here for Ellie, not me. I cared about Sal as a friend, but there's a part of me that can't forgive her.'

Cass could think of a number of unforgivable things that Sal had done, but tact got the better of her. 'What for?'

'I'd hoped that when Sal got back from Nepal, we might be able to come to some arrangement so that Ellie would have a proper family. I was prepared to do anything to make that happen.'

'But…surely that wasn't her fault. She died…'

'Yeah. She never told me that she was going to Everest without the proper permits or a place on an expedition. It was just plain crazy and I would have stopped her if I'd known.'

Jack took a last look at the photograph. 'I didn't have the time with my father that I wanted, but at least I knew him. Ellie doesn't even have that; she doesn't remember Sal at all.'

'Ellie seems…' Cass tried to concentrate on something else '…very happy. Very secure.' She remembered seeing Jack hug Ellie when he'd left, and then, in a moment of stillness between the two, he'd put his hand on his heart. Ellie had mimicked him and then let him go without any tears.

'She knows I'll always come back for her.' He shrugged. 'But sometimes I wish…' He shook his head, as if wishes couldn't possibly come true.

Cass hardly dared ask. But she did, anyway. 'What do you wish?'

A sudden heat in his eyes, which turned from fierce intensity to something warmer. 'I miss being able to ask a woman out to dinner.' The tips of his fingers were almost touching her arm. Almost reaching for her, but not quite.

'And you can't do that?' There were plenty of single fathers that did.

'I reckon that the one thing that's worse for Ellie than not having a mother is having a succession of temporary ones. I can't let her lose any more than she already has. I wish it were different, but…'

'Yeah. I miss…' The warmth of having someone. The tingling sense of excitement every time Jack walked into a room had made her realise just how much she missed that.

'But aren't you married to your work?' He raised an eye-brow. 'You're not thinking of getting a divorce, are you?'

'No. That relationship's doing just fine, thank you.'

'Shame.'

The thought that maybe, just maybe, there was another option left her breathless. If they both knew that nothing could come of it, if no one ever knew, then there couldn't be any hurt. If neither of them expected anything, then surely neither of them could be disappointed.

Maybe it wasn't quite that simple. Jack had just the kind of body, just the kind of touch, which made sex for the sake of it seem like the best idea she'd had in years. But there was more to him than that, and his tenderness could make things very complicated.

She turned away from him, breaking the spell. 'We should get going if we want to get back to the village and then make another round trip this afternoon.'

Maybe her disappointment sounded in her voice. He smiled then caught up the bag that lay in the doorway, ushering her outside and then slinging his coat across his shoulders to run to the car.

# CHAPTER EIGHT

As soon as they got back to the village they started on the round of visits that Jack had promised to make, Cass acting as his guide. The first on the list was Mr Hughes. He had refused to allow his wife to stay and watch while Jack checked on his pacemaker, and Mrs Hughes had refused to stay in the kitchen, so Cass waited outside the sitting room door with her.

'I really don't know why he didn't go to the hospital sooner. He missed his last appointment, and they said that he had to go in three months. He hasn't got much left on the battery...'

Cass nodded sympathetically, wondering when Mrs Hughes was going to stop with the barrage of complaints about her husband.

'Then, all of a sudden, it gets to be urgent and we can't go because of the floods.' Mrs Hughes gave a derisive sniff. 'Silly man. I wish he'd look after himself a bit better. I do my best.'

'I'm sure it'll all be okay.' Cass ventured some reassurance, based rather more on Jack's expertise than what she knew about Mr Hughes' lifestyle.

'He doesn't listen to me. I've told him more times...' Mrs Hughes broke off as Jack emerged from the sitting room. Behind him, Mr Hughes looked suitably chastened.

'I'm taking your husband's results to the hospital this afternoon.' He gave Mrs Hughes a smile and she brightened immediately.

'And…?'

'His consultant will review them and give you a call. There's nothing to worry about; his pacemaker is doing its job and there are no problems there, but I think that Mr Hughes may well benefit from taking a few measures to improve his general health.'

'Thank you, Doctor.' Mrs Hughes shot a look of triumph at her husband.

'I'm a paramedic.'

Mrs Hughes leaned towards Jack confidingly. 'I don't care who you are. Just as long as you told him…'

Jack nodded, clearly unwilling to commit himself about what he had or hadn't told Mr Hughes, and Mrs Hughes saw them to the front door. Cass followed him down the front path and fell in step with him.

'More exercise. Give up smoking and change his diet…'

Jack grinned. 'Very good. You want to take the next visit?'

Cass shook her head. 'Everyone in the village knows. I imagine the only person who *doesn't* know is the consultant at the hospital. When I asked Mrs Hughes if she'd spoken to him, she said she didn't like to.'

'Why not?'

Cass shrugged. 'Because he's far too important. And clearly far too busy to be worrying about his patients' health.'

Jack gave a resigned groan. 'Okay. He's actually a good man, and very approachable. I'll be making the situation clear in my notes and he'll follow up.'

'Thanks.' Cass swerved off the road and climbed over a stile, jumping down on the other side. 'Short cut.'

Jack had almost completely lost his bearings. Here, on

the other side of the village from the river, the land sloped more gently and houses were scattered between fields and copses of trees. The ring of water that surrounded the area spread out into the distance, encroaching wherever it could through gullies and streams and into homes. But Cass seemed to know every inch of the place, and so far they hadn't even got their feet wet.

'Any other bits of interesting gossip I should know about?' It sounded as if the villagers knew who needed medical help long before anyone else did.

'Don't think so. Joe Gardener pulled a muscle yesterday, carrying my kitchen door.'

'He mentioned that last night when I saw him. The tube of vapour rub from the chemist is for him. What about you?'

'Me? Nothing wrong with me.'

Jack had expected her to say that. But he'd heard a little village gossip too, last night. 'It's just that if there was someone who'd been up all night on more than one occasion in the past few weeks, who'd been holding down a physically demanding job, digging ditches and looking after a pregnant sister...'

She shot him a warning glare, compressing her lips into a hard line. Jack ignored it.

'...rescuing kids, and then going through the trauma of having her own house flooded, I'd be a bit concerned.'

'Would you, now?'

'Do you want to talk about it?'

She stopped short, almost tripping over a tree root when she turned to face him. 'What's all this about, Jack? I'm fine. I told you.'

'Okay. Just asking.' If she wasn't going to talk about it, then he couldn't make her. 'But if you do need anything.'

'So I'm needy now, am I?' She frowned at him.

'No. You might be human, though. And if it turns out that you are, and you need a friend...' He shrugged. Why should she turn to him? She was surrounded by friends here and she never seemed to want to take any help from anyone.

Suddenly she seemed to soften. 'Jack, I...' She shook her head and the moment was lost. 'Will you do something for me? As a friend.'

'Of course.'

'Will you just shut up?'

He'd obviously gone too far and Cass was withdrawn and quiet as they circled the low-lying areas of the village, dropping off prescriptions and visiting anyone who might need medical support. But, whatever sadness she concealed, and Jack was sure by now that she was hiding something, she never hung on to it for long. Cass was nothing if not resilient, and by the time they'd walked back up the hill to Miss Palmer's cottage, she was smiling again.

'I can't wait to see what Bathsheba's going to get up to next.' Cass grinned at Miss Palmer. While Jack had been checking her over and doing the INR test, Cass had produced an MP3 player from her pocket and plugged it into a laptop which lay on a side table.

'Oh, I think you'll be surprised.' Miss Palmer smiled enigmatically.

'Miss Palmer's reading Thomas Hardy. I can read it myself, but it's easier when she does it for me.'

'You can concentrate on what's happening, you mean?' Jack liked the idea, and it obviously gave both Cass and Miss Palmer a lot of pleasure.

'Yes. I get to enjoy the story.'

'It's our little secret.' Miss Palmer was looking at him speculatively, and Jack was learning never to ignore any of Miss Palmer's looks. 'Just between the two of us. Or the three of us, I suppose.'

Cass's cheeks flushed a little, but she didn't seem to mind. And Jack had the sudden feeling that the brick wall that Cass had built around herself had just crumbled a little. Not so much as to allow him to see over the top, but if he put his shoulder to it a few more times who knew what might happen?

They'd retraced their route back along the flooded motorway and to Cass's car. She'd waited in the hospital car park for him, plugging the MP3 player into the car's sound system while Jack returned the borrowed equipment and made sure that the results of the tests he'd taken would reach the right people.

'What time does Ellie go to bed?' When he climbed back into the SUV, she looked at her watch.

'In about half an hour. But if we go now, we'll get back across the water while it's still light.' Jack knew what she was thinking. He'd been thinking the same himself, but it was too late now.

She started the engine. 'Won't take long to kiss her goodnight, will it? And I've got a flashlight in the back of the car.'

'Anything you *don't* have in the back of your car?'

She chuckled. 'I like to come prepared.'

They were in time for Jack to put Ellie to bed. He walked back downstairs to find Cass alone in the sitting room, still listening to her MP3 player.

'Ready?'

'Yeah. Thanks.' He said a quick goodbye to Sarah, resisting the temptation to go and wake Ellie up, just to say goodnight to her again, and followed Cass to her car.

When they arrived at the motorway, she pulled a large flashlight from the car boot, switching it on. It illuminated the water in front of them as she swung it slowly.

'They must not be here yet.' There was no answering flash of light from the gloom on the other side. 'They won't be long.'

Suddenly, the men coming to fetch them could be as long as they liked. It could rain as much as it liked. Jack reached for her, wondering whether she would back away.

She didn't. Cass took a step towards him, the beam of the flashlight swaying suddenly upwards. They were touching now. Sweaters and coats between them, but still nothing to protect him from the intoxicating magic that she exuded.

'Switch it off.' His own voice sounded hoarse, almost abrupt.

An answering snap, and they were standing in semi-darkness. She pulled down her hood, rain splashing on to her face as she tipped it up towards him.

'Cassandra...' Jack had already lost sight of all the reasons why he shouldn't do this. All the things that stood between them seemed to have melted away.

'Jack...?' There were so many questions in the dark shadows of her eyes and he couldn't answer any of them.

'Yes?'

'...Nothing.' She whispered the word, her lips curving into a tantalising smile.

He was confused, torn apart by two equal forces pulling in opposite directions. Cass was the only thing that seemed real, the only thing he could take hold of and hang on to. He pulled her close, hearing the soft thud as the flashlight hit the grass at their feet.

# CHAPTER NINE

HIS BODY WAS as strong, as delicious as she'd imagined it. When he held her there was no possibility of escape, unless he decided to free her. But Cass didn't want to be free of him.

Still he seemed to hesitate. Going slow, waiting for her to stop him. That wasn't going to happen. She pulled his hood back, laying her hands on either side of his face.

She could feel him breathe. Then he said her name again. 'Cassandra.'

'I'm right here, Jack.'

He touched his lips against hers, soft and gentle. That wasn't what she wanted and he knew it. When he came back for more, the sudden intensity made her legs wobble. Pinpricks of cool water on her face and the raging heat of his kiss. It was almost too much, but at the same time she didn't want it to end.

Layers of heavy-duty, high-performance waterproofing scraped together as he lifted her off her feet. Cass wrapped her legs around his waist and her arms around his shoulders, looking down into his eyes now. His hand on the back of her head brought her lips to his, their kiss annihilating her.

He could lay her on the grass... Suddenly the rain and layers of clothing meant nothing. The possibility that they might be discovered meant nothing. Nothing meant anything as long as he could find a way to touch her, in all the places that she wanted him to.

'Jack…' She moved against him so desperately that he almost lost his footing.

'Careful.' He nuzzled against her neck, the warmth of his lips against the cold rivulets of water that trickled from her wet hair. One hand cupped her bottom, supporting her, and the other seemed to be burrowing inside her jacket. Then she felt his fingers, cool on her spine, just above the waistband of her jeans.

His touch made her breath catch in her throat. Caressing, tantalising. If he could do that with one square inch of naked skin to work with, then goodness only knew what he might do with more.

Then, suddenly, he stopped. 'Cass… Cass, we have company…'

'Uh?' *No!*

'Feet on the ground, honey.' His voice was gentle, holding all the promise of what might have been if fantasy had any power to hold off reality. She slowly planted her boots back down on to the grass, feeling his body against hers, supporting her until she felt able to stand. When she turned, she saw lights tracing a path down towards where the dinghy was kept.

'Too bad…' She picked up the flashlight and switched it on, signalling to the group on the other side of the water.

His fingers found hers, curling around them. 'Yeah. I can't imagine…'

'Can't you?' She smiled up at him.

'Actually, I can. I'm imagining it right now.' He bent towards her slightly. 'What I'd do…'

'Don't. Jack…' Her skin suddenly seemed to have developed a mind of its own and was tingling, as if responding to his touch.

'What you'd do.'

'Jack, I'm warning you…'

'Yeah. I'll consider myself well and truly warned.' He squeezed her hand and then let it go, one last brush of his finger against her palm making her shiver. Lights shone across the dark water and the sound of the dinghy's motor reached her ears. And Jack's smile beside her, indicating that in his mind he was still touching her.

It was easy to tell himself that it had been a delicious one-off moment in time that wasn't going to happen again, when there was so little chance of he and Cass being left alone for long. They'd missed supper and ate in a corner of the kitchen, the bustle of clearing up after the evening meal going on around them. And afterwards there were people waiting to see Cass, to discuss plans for shoring up the makeshift dams which were keeping the water away from a number of houses in the village.

She didn't once mention her own house. A few times, Jack saw her press her lips together in an expression of regret over something she didn't want to talk about and he wondered whether he might get her alone, later. But by the time the meeting broke up, everyone was yawning, Cass included, and clearly they were all off to their own beds.

He hadn't kissed a woman since Ellie had come into his life. Maybe that was why he couldn't stop thinking about last night. Jack felt a quiver of guilt as he made his way to the church hall the following morning and deliberately slowed his pace. He shouldn't be so eager just to get a glimpse of Cass.

'Watch out!' A burly man in a red waterproof jacket cannoned straight into him as he walked through the lobby, and then shouted the warning in his face.

'Sorry, mate.' Jack stepped back as the man staggered a little. 'You all right?'

'Yeah. Sorry. Splitting headache this morning.' The man stopped and seemed to collect himself. 'Must be a stomach bug. The wife and kids have got it too; when I left, my youngest boy was throwing up.'

'Yeah? You need anything?'

'No, it's okay. The walk here seems to be clearing it.'

A slight prickling at the back of Jack's neck. It was probably nothing but he asked anyway, keeping his tone conversational. 'Any other families got it?'

'Not that I know of.' The man straightened. 'The power's off at my place and it gets cold at night, even though we keep the heater on in the hall. Probably just a stuffy head from too many blankets.' He took off his coat, hanging it with the others, and opened the hall door to let Jack through.

Cass was easy to pick out immediately, her red hair shining like a beacon that seemed to draw him in. Jack reminded himself that he had more important concerns at the moment, and that wanting to touch her could wait.

'Can I have a word?' He motioned her to one side. 'The guy in the brown sweater who's just arrived.'

Cass looked round. 'The one with the beard? That's Frank.'

'Where does he live?'

'Over on the other side of the village.' She shot him a questioning look. 'What's the matter?'

'Have you heard about anyone else with a stomach bug? Headaches, sickness?'

'No. We all know about the dangers of flood water, if that's what you're getting at. Everyone's drinking bottled.' She paused. 'The whole family usually comes up here for breakfast; the power's out down there.'

'He was on his own this morning. And he says that all of the family have had headaches and sickness, which clears in the open air.'

'You don't think...?' As a firefighter, Cass probably knew the symptoms of carbon monoxide poisoning better than he did.

'I don't know.'

'Best make sure.'

They found their coats, and Jack quickly packed a few things that he hoped he wouldn't need into a small rucksack. Cass led the way, turning away from the river, taking the path they'd taken yesterday. He wondered whether he should mention last night to her, perhaps even apologise, but Cass had already pulled her phone from her pocket and was scrolling through the contact list.

'No answer. Maybe they're on their way up to the church.' Even so, she quickened her pace, striding along the perimeter of a field of corn, the crop rotting where it stood. On the far side they slid down a steep incline and then back on to the road.

Cass had called again and there was still no answer. She and Jack almost ran the few feet along the road and then up the path of a large modern house. She banged on the door, bending down to look through the letter box.

'Someone's coming.'

The door was answered by a heavy-eyed lad of about eighteen. 'Cass?' He shielded his eyes against the light. 'What is it?'

'This is Jack; he's a paramedic. Can we come in, please, Harry?'

'Yeah. If you're looking for Mum, she's not very well. She and Alex have gone back to bed.'

'Are you okay?'

'Not too bad. I went out for a walk this morning and it cleared my head. But it's so stuffy in here...' The lad shrugged, standing back from the doorway and eyeing Jack. 'I heard all about you...'

It seemed that most of the village had heard all about

him, and at the moment that was a good thing because he could dispense with the usual formalities. Jack walked straight into the house and up the stairs.

Behind him, he could hear Cass telling Harry to wait in the hallway. There was a portable gas heater on the landing, which looked as if it had been hauled out of the garden shed and pressed into service when the power failed. Jack reached out, turning it off as he passed.

The first of the back bedrooms was in darkness, and from the mess of posters on the wall its occupant must be fifteen or sixteen. Jack opened the curtains and a drowsy protest came from the bed.

'Geroff. My head…'

'Alex, my name's Jack. I'm a paramedic. Get up.' Jack didn't bother with any niceties. He stripped the duvet off the bed and the dark-haired youth protested.

His speech was so slurred that Jack wasn't entirely sure what he was saying, but it sounded like a none-too-polite request to go away and leave him alone. He hauled the youth up on to his feet, pulling his arm around his neck. 'Walk. Come on.'

Jack supported the boy over to the bedroom door. He was showing all the signs of having flu—flushed cheeks, drowsiness and, from the way he was clutching one hand to his head, a headache. But flu didn't get better when you went out for a walk in the fresh air, and carbon monoxide poisoning did.

'Coming through…' Cass's voice on the landing. She was carrying a woman in the classic fireman's lift, her body coiled around her shoulders. She looked to be unresponsive.

'Harry, get out of the way!' Cass called to the lad, who was now halfway up the stairs, and he turned and ran back down again.

'Mum…? What's the matter?' He flattened himself

against the wall of the hallway, letting Cass past to the front door, and Jack followed.

'Harry… What's going on?' The boy at Jack's side grabbed at his brother.

'You'll be okay, but you need to get into the fresh air. Now.' Jack tried to reassure the panicking boys. He seized a couple of coats from the pegs in the hall and thrust them at Harry.

Harry transitioned suddenly from a boy to a man. 'Go on and help Mum. I'll see to Alex.'

Jack followed Cass out of the front door and she led the way round to the car port at the side of the house, where there was at least some protection from the rain. He tore off his coat, wrapping it around the woman as Cass lay her carefully down.

'Her name's Sylvie.'

'Thanks. Will you fetch my bag, please?' Sylvie's breathing was a little too shallow for Jack's liking, but at least she was breathing. Her eyelids were fluttering and she seemed lost somewhere between consciousness and unconsciousness. Cass nodded and a moment later the rucksack was laid down on the concrete next to him.

'Oxygen?' She anticipated his next instruction, opening the bag and taking out the small oxygen cylinder.

'Thanks. Can you see to the boys? And try and knock for a neighbour; this isn't ideal.'

'Right you are.' Cass disappeared and Jack held the oxygen mask to Sylvie's mouth. 'Sylvie… Sylvie, open your eyes.'

A figure knelt down on the concrete on the other side of the prone body. Harry picked up his mother's hand, his face set and calm. 'Mum…'

'That's right. Talk to her.' Jack knew that Sylvie would

respond to her son's voice better than his. He cradled her, holding the mask over her face.

'Mum... Come on now, wake up.' Jack allowed himself a grim smile. Harry's voice was firm and steady. 'Open your eyes, Mum. Come on.'

Sylvie's eyes opened and Jack felt her begin to retch. Quickly he bent her forward and she was sick all over the leg of her son's jeans. 'Nice one, Mum.' Harry didn't flinch. 'Better out than in...'

Jack grinned, clearing Sylvie's mouth and letting her lie back in his arms. She opened her eyes and her gaze found her son's face.

'Harry...I feel so ill...'

'I know, Mum. But Cass and the paramedic are here, and you're going to be okay.'

'Alex...'

'He's okay. He's gone with Cass.' Harry stroked his mother's brow.

'I'm going to put a mask over your face, Sylvie. Deep breaths.' Jack replaced the mask, and Sylvie's chest rose and fell as she breathed in the oxygen.

'That's right, Mum.' Harry's gaze flickered towards Jack and he nodded him on. 'Deep breaths, eh. Do as the man says.'

'Well done.' Jack didn't take his gaze from Sylvie but the words were for Harry. 'You just passed the first responder's initiation. Don't back off when someone's sick all over you.'

The young man gave a nervous laugh. 'What the hell's the matter with her...? With us?'

'I think it may be carbon monoxide poisoning. She seems to be coming out of it now.' Sylvie was quiet but her eyes were open and focused.

'What...like car exhaust fumes?'

'Something like that. One of those heaters may be faulty. Where did you get them?'

'Dad's mate lent them to us. He uses them in his greenhouse.'

Sylvie stirred in his arms and Jack smiled down at her. 'All right. You're doing just fine, Sylvie.'

Cass knelt down beside him. 'Next door. They're waiting for us.'

'Thanks. Help me lift her?' Jack gave the oxygen tank to Harry to carry, more as a badge of honour than anything else, and Cass helped settle Sylvie in his arms. A middle-aged woman was standing at the door of the next house, and Jack carried Sylvie carefully up her own front path and back down her neighbour's.

The house was neat and warm. He was waved through to a sitting room, two large sofas placed on opposite sides of the room. On one sat a man, his arm clamped tightly around Alex's shoulders.

'She's all right, Alex. She just needs fresh air and she'll be okay. We all will.' Harry seemed to have taken over Jack's role and he relinquished it gladly to him. When this was all over the young man could feel proud of the way he'd acted.

He laid Sylvie gently down on the sofa. A roll of kitchen towel was produced, to wipe Harry's jeans, and Jack asked him to sit with his mother. Cass appeared from the hallway, pocketing her phone.

'You'll be wanting her seen at the hospital?'

'Yeah. All of them need to have blood tests for carbon monoxide.'

'Okay, there are a couple of cars coming now, and we'll take them down to the motorway and get them across there. A lot quicker than calling an ambulance...' She stopped suddenly, reddening. 'What do you think?'

'I think we'd better get a couple of cars down here and take them across at the motorway. It'll be a lot quicker than calling an ambulance.' His eyes sparkled with amusement.

'Yeah. Right.' Cass wrinkled her nose at him and Jack tried not to laugh. She was irresistible when she second-guessed him, and that thing with the nose was the icing on the cake.

'How long?' He had to make a conscious effort to get his mind back on to the task in hand.

'Ten minutes. I'll go and get some clothes for them.'

'Just coats, from the hallway.' The front door must be still open and the air in the hallway would have cleared by now. 'I don't want to have to carry *you* out.' Though he'd carry her pretty much anywhere she liked if given half a chance.

'I'd like to see you try.' She turned her back on him and marched out of the room, leaving him to his patient.

# CHAPTER TEN

SYLVIE'S HUSBAND WAS in one of the cars that arrived and the family was ferried down to the motorway together. Cass had disappeared, and Jack saw her waiting on the other side of the water with her SUV. She dropped the keys into Jack's hand and told him she'd meet him at the hospital and Jack helped Sylvie into the front seat, the rest of the family squeezing into the back.

He drove away, leaving her standing alone on the road. There wasn't any point in wondering exactly how she was going to get to the hospital. She'd said she'd be there, and Jack had little doubt that she would.

She arrived, pink-cheeked, nearly an hour later and sat down next to him on one of the waiting room chairs.

'Hey.'

'Hey yourself.' He wasn't going to ask.

'Everything all right?'

'Fine. They're being seen now.' Jack reached into his pocket and took out her car keys. 'Blue.'

'Blue?'

'When Sylvie was called in I nipped out and put your car through the car wash around the corner. Just in case you happened to be looking for it, it's blue.'

She gave him a sweet smile, refusing to rise to the bait. 'I'll bear that in mind. Thanks.'

They sat in silence for a few minutes. Cass took off her coat and dropped it on the chair next to her.

'You could at least ask.'

Jack smirked. He'd been determined that she would be the first to break. 'All right. How did you get here?'

'I walked for about a mile and then I hitched a lift. On the mobility bus.'

Jack snorted with laughter. 'The mobility bus? Didn't they want to see your pensioner's card before they let you on?'

'No, they did not. I showed the firefighter's ID card I have for home safety checks and cadged a lift.'

'And said you were on your way to a fire?' This was the first opportunity he'd had to sit and talk alone with Cass since they'd kissed. It felt almost as if he'd been holding his breath, waiting for this moment.

'Very funny. Next time *you* have a fire, don't expect me to put it out.' She turned her head away from him and Jack saw that she was blushing furiously at her own gaffe.

'I can put out my own fires, thank you.' Something about the delicate pink of her pale skin just wouldn't allow him to let this go. That, and the thought of letting her put out the delicious fire that her kiss had ignited.

She turned, grinning at him, and Jack suddenly wondered what he'd just got himself into. 'You're no fun, are you?'

That smile. Those dark eyes, full of all the things that might have been last night. She hadn't stopped thinking about it. It had been running at the back of her mind, like a piece of music playing over and over on the radio. Unnoticed for most of the time, but still there.

Maybe she should just get a grip. Put Jack away in a box, lined with tissue paper, ready to take back out again when she was old and grey and wanted to remind herself of what it was like to be young.

'That was a nice lift. Good technique.' He spoke quietly, almost daring her to rise to the challenge.

'Thanks. One of those things that firefighters do.' She shot him a smile, daring him back.

'Better than paramedics, you mean?'

'Much better.'

He was unashamedly sizing her up. Cass returned the compliment. Jack was a good deal heavier than her, but she'd lifted men before. It was all a matter of technique. And the stubbornness to give it a go. Right now she'd do practically anything to avoid thinking about the responsibilities waiting for her back at the village.

He heaved a sigh, as if his next question had already been asked and answered. 'Car park?'

Cass nodded. 'Car park.'

Jack popped his head into the treatment area, checking that the family weren't ready to go yet, and they walked silently out of A and E.

'You're sure about this, now?' He was strolling next to her, his hands in his pockets.

No, she wasn't sure at all. Not about any of it. Cass stopped between two cars and stood in close, putting her right leg in between his, trying to imagine that he was a practice dummy. It wasn't working.

'Mind your back.' He chose this moment to grin at her and offer advice. Cass ignored it.

Grabbing his right arm, she positioned it over her left shoulder. Then, in one fluid movement, she bent her knees, wound her left arm around the back of his leg and lifted him off his feet.

'There. Easy.' She felt him put his free hand on the small of her back, balancing his weight and steadying her. It wasn't quite as easy as she was making out, but she could walk a dozen steps before she swung him back down on to his feet.

'Impressive.' He looked impressed as well. Some men would object to a woman being able to carry them, others might suffer it in silence, but she'd never imagined that it might be a cause for congratulation. But then Jack was different to most men.

Or perhaps he wasn't. His lips curled, and suddenly she was pressed hard up against him, his leg between hers. 'Hey...!'

'Sorry. That's not right, is it?' He eased back a bit, turning what felt a lot like an embrace into the exact position for a lift. Then she found herself swung up on to his shoulders with about as much effort as it would have taken to swat a fly.

His right arm was wound around the back of her knee, his hand holding her arm. Perfect form. Perfect balance.

'Not bad.'

He chuckled. 'What's wrong with it?'

What was wrong with it was that the primitive beat of her heart actually wanted him to carry her off to his lair and claim her as his. He'd lifted her with no apparent effort last night, and she'd always assumed that he was perfectly capable of slinging her over his shoulder, but having him do it was something different.

'You're not running.'

He settled her weight on his shoulders and started to stroll slowly back to A and E. 'Paramedics never run when they can walk. We don't go in for all that macho firefighter stuff.'

'Cheek!' She smacked at his back with her free hand. 'Are you calling me macho?'

'Never. Takes a real woman to do what you do.'

She tapped his shoulder. 'Thinking of letting me down any time soon?' She was getting to like this far too much.

His scent, the feel of his body. The sudden dizzy feeling that accompanied his compliments.

'Oh. Yeah, of course.' He didn't bend to set her back down on her feet, just shifted her around so that she slithered to the ground against his body.

'You lost marks there.' She stared up into his eyes.

'I know. Worth it, though.'

It was the most exquisite kind of letting go. Forgetting about the effort and the stress of the morning and taking something for themselves, even if it was just messing around in a car park, testing each other's strength. And if it meant any more than that, Cass was going to choose to ignore it.

'Suppose we should get back.' He nodded and they started back towards the hospital building. Back towards the cares of the day, the problems that still needed to be solved. And still neither of them had said anything about the one thing that she couldn't stop thinking about. That kiss.

The smell of a Sunday roast pervaded the church hall and people were busy smoothing tablecloths and positioning cutlery. Everything neat and tidy, as if the families of Holme were determined to show themselves, and each other, that despite everything which had been thrown at them in the last few weeks, life went on.

Jack popped his head around the kitchen door to ask what time lunch would be, fully expecting to be shooed away, but instead he was drawn in and questioned rigorously about Sylvie and her family. He imparted the news that they were all recovering well, that Sylvie was spending tonight under observation in the hospital and that the family would stay with her sister in town. In return, he was told that no one knew where Cass was, but that she'd gone out about half an hour ago, saying she wouldn't be long.

Armed with half a packet of biscuits, and the knowledge

that it would be another hour before lunch was served, he walked through the winding passageways at the back of the church, losing his way a couple of times, but finally managing to find the corridor that led to the porch. When he opened the door, no one was there.

He wondered whether he should sit down and wait for Cass. This was her private place and it seemed like an intrusion, but he needed to talk to her alone.

He had to make a choice. He could leave, and thank his lucky stars that the constant demands of other people had meant that one brief but sensational kiss was all they'd been able to share. Or he could live with that mistake and not let it stop him from doing the right thing.

He heard footsteps approaching the door. When she opened the door into the porch she was rubbing her face, as if supremely weary. In that moment, Jack knew that he cared about her far too much to leave her here, with such a heavy weight of responsibility on her shoulders.

'Jack!' As soon as she caught sight of him she seemed to rally herself. 'What's the matter?'

'Nothing.'

She shot him a puzzled look, then dropped the pair of waders she was holding and took off her coat.

'Where have you been?' She pressed her lips together in reply and Jack gave up trying to pretend that he didn't know. 'Your house?'

'Yeah.'

Jack swallowed the temptation to say that if she'd told him he would have gone with her. 'What's it like down there?'

She sat down, clearly trying not to look at him. 'Wet. Pretty dismal.'

'And how are you feeling?'

Cass gave a grim smile. 'Pretty dismal too.'

He leaned across, handing her the packet of biscuits. 'Chocolate digestive?' It was little enough, but at least she took them.

She unwrapped the packet, her fingers clumsy, as if she were numb. 'What are these for?'

'I want to talk to you. I reckoned that offering you food might keep you in one place for a minute.'

She pulled a biscuit out of the packet, the ghost of a smile playing around her lips. 'You have my undivided attention.' She waved the biscuit. 'Almost.'

Jack smiled at her. It wasn't much of a joke, but then she must be feeling pretty horrible right now. 'You're going back to work tomorrow? Your fire station's the one in town, isn't it?'

She nodded. 'Yeah. Early start. I'm trying not to think about it.'

She was going to *have* to think about it tomorrow. Trying to use the showers without waking everyone else up. Getting across the water, alone and in the chill darkness of an early morning. Arriving at work already exhausted. Jack tried one last gambit before he suggested the only other solution he could think of. 'You don't have anywhere you can stay in town? A friend?'

'Normally I would. But there are so many people flooded out that no one's got any room at the moment.'

'I live pretty close to town. You could stay with me and Ellie.' Including Ellie in the invitation might make it sound a little less as if he was trying to make a pass at her. 'I have a spare room so you'd have your own space.'

She stared at him blankly. 'My own space?'

'Yeah.' Saying that the kiss had meant nothing was far too big a lie to even contemplate. 'Last night is…then. And today is…'

'Now…?' Tension hovered in the air between them and

clearly Cass knew exactly what he was talking about. Perhaps she'd been thinking about it too.

'Yeah. Then and now. Concentrate on now.'

She shook her head slowly. 'I appreciate the offer. But I should stay here.'

'Cass, you know that's not going to work. Goodness only knows how long it'll take you to get to work from here. You'll do a demanding job, then come back here and find there are a load of other problems to deal with. It's too much and you know it.'

'I can manage.' Her voice was flat, measured. Jack knew that she was close to breaking point and if pushing her a little further was what it took to make her see sense...

'No, actually, you can't manage. This village owes you a great deal. But no one wants you here now. You need a break, and if you don't take it then you'll make a mistake. You and I can't afford to make mistakes, not in our jobs.'

Shock registered in her eyes and then she twisted her mouth in a parody of a grin. 'Kick a girl when she's down, why don't you.'

'If that's what it takes.' He'd resolved that he wouldn't touch her, that he'd demonstrate that he could keep his distance. But even a friend would offer comfort. Jack shifted over to sit next to her and wrapped one arm tightly around her shoulder. He might not have managed to persuade Cass, but he'd persuaded himself. Leaving her behind was totally out of the question.

He always seemed so warm. So solid. And she still felt as if the ground had been whipped out from under her feet, after the shock of wading through the dirty water that was almost a foot deep in the ground floor of her house.

'I suppose...' She shifted a little, wondering if he'd let her go, and gratifyingly he didn't take the hint. 'I suppose you're going to say that I don't have any other choice.'

'Nah.' He rested his chin lightly on the top of her head. 'I'm not going to waste my breath by telling you what you already know.'

Even now, he made her smile. If close proximity to Jack was hard, then continuing on here without him would be harder still. And since he seemed so intent on disregarding the kiss, then she could too. She could turn a blind eye to the clutter of Ellie's things around her and resist the temptation to pick the little girl up and hold her to her heart.

'Maybe just a couple of days. You won't know I'm there...'

'You can make as much noise and as much mess as you like. That's one of the rules of the house.'

Cass thought for a moment. 'I cook...'

'Great. Knock yourself out. We can take it in turns; I wouldn't mind a few evenings off.'

He had an answer for everything. And right now Cass couldn't see any further than a hot meal and a night's sleep, uninterrupted by worry. She straightened, disentangling herself from his arms, and Jack moved back quickly.

'Okay. Thanks.'

As soon as Jack made up his mind to do something, he just did it. No messing around, no fuss. Martin would keep an eye on her house while she was gone, and she was assured time and time again that she was doing the right thing. Jack had quietly overseen everything, and if the feeling that the whole village was handing her over to him was a little strange it wasn't a bad one.

Lunch had been eaten and Martin had stood up to make a brief speech, sending them on their way with the thanks and good wishes of the community. Hugs had been exchanged and they'd walked out into the sunshine.

'Not giving me a chance to change my mind?' Jack had propelled Cass firmly into the car that was waiting outside.

'May as well go now, while the rain holds off.' He shot her a sizzling grin. 'And I'm not giving you the chance to change your mind.'

By the time they reached his house, it was raining again. Jack showed her up to the spare room, told her to make herself at home and disappeared to collect Ellie, leaving Cass to sit on the bed and draw breath for the first time in what seemed like for ever.

She looked around. The room was clearly hardly used, meticulously tidy and a little chilly from having the door closed and the heating turned off. But it was bright and comfortable and, for the next few days, it was her space.

It was quiet too. After the bustle of the vicarage and the church hall, this seemed like heaven. She listened at the silence for a while. Maybe this hadn't been such a bad idea after all.

## CHAPTER ELEVEN

THE EVENING HAD passed in a welter of good manners and keeping their distance. The next morning was rather less formal, on account of the rush to get Ellie up and both of them out of the house in time for work, but Jack reckoned that they were doing okay. Then he got the phone call.

He'd picked Ellie up from Sarah's in a daze of misery. Done his best to pretend that there was nothing wrong, until after he'd tucked Ellie in and kissed her goodnight. When he went back downstairs, the house was quiet.

'What's the matter?' Cass was sitting on the edge of one of the armchairs, looking at him thoughtfully.

'Nothing. Long day.' She'd come here for a break. He didn't want to burden her with his problems.

'Don't do that to me. I told you mine, and now you can tell me yours. That's the deal, Jack, and if you don't like it then I'm out.'

In that moment, Jack knew that this was all that he'd wanted. Someone to come home to. Someone he could share this with.

'It's Mimi. She's been hurt.'

'When?'

Jack slumped down onto the sofa. 'Yesterday afternoon. I heard about it this morning; Rafe called me when I was on my way to work. I went straight in to see how she was...'

He closed his eyes, the lump in his throat preventing him from saying any more.

The sofa cushions moved as Cass sat down beside him. 'And how is she?'

'She's in the ICU. None of her injuries are life-threatening, but she's in a bad way. I went up at lunchtime and they let me sit with her for half an hour.'

'Is she awake?'

He shook his head. 'It's better they keep her under sedation for a while.'

'Would you like to go back now? I'll stay here and look after Ellie.'

'There's no point. They won't let me in, and there's nothing I can do. Rafe's promised to phone if there's any change.'

He felt her fingers touch the back of his hand and he pulled away from her. That wasn't going to help. Nothing was going to help.

'What is it, Jack?'

'You think that this isn't enough?' He heard anger flare in his voice and it shocked him. When he glared at Cass, she flushed, pressing her lips together. Now wasn't the time for her to clam up on him.

'Just say it, Cass. You really can't make anything any worse.'

'Things could be a lot worse and you know it. Since when did you give up on anyone, Jack?'

'I am *not*...' The denial sprang to Jack's lips before he realised that Cass had seen a lot more than he had. Giving up on Mimi was exactly what he was doing.

All he wanted her to do was hold him. Maybe she saw that too because she reached across, taking his shaking hands between hers. Jack could never imagine that Cass's touch could be anything other than exciting, but now it was soothing.

'I'm afraid of losing her, Cass. She went into a building and it flooded…' He shook his head. 'Why did she have to go and do that?'

'Same reason you would, I imagine. This isn't really about Mimi, is it?'

Cass always seemed to see right through him, and right now it was the only thing that could bring him any comfort. 'I was so angry with my father when he died. I felt he cared more about getting off on the risk than he did about us. Sal too…'

Cass let go of his hands, curling her arms around his shoulders. Jack hung on to her as tightly as if he were drowning.

'I'd be angry too. But you have to forget that now because Mimi's your friend and she deserves your trust. You have to believe in her.'

She'd cut right to the heart of it. To his heart. The thought that once again he might lose someone who was important in his life had torn at him all day. He hadn't been able to see past his anger, hadn't even allowed himself to feel any hope for Mimi.

'I let her down, didn't I?'

'No. And you're not going to either, because you're going back to the ICU tomorrow and you're going to tell her how much you care about her, and that you know she's going to get better. Even if she can't hear you.'

'Perhaps she can. You always have to assume that even heavily sedated patients can hear what's going on.'

'Well, in that case you'd better make it convincing.' The flicker of a smile caressed her lips. 'Go on. Let's see your convincing face.'

She could make him laugh even when things were bad. She might not be able to make all the worry disappear, nor could she drive away all the simmering fear and anger, but she knew how to give him hope. Jack gave an approximation of his most earnest expression and she shook her head, laughing.

'I'd stick with the one you gave Lynette. I wouldn't buy a used car off you if you looked at me like that.'

She made him a drink, and got a smile in return, but she could still feel the pain leaking out of him. He wasn't just dealing with Mimi being hurt; he was dealing with all of the remembered pain of his father's death. All of the fears he had for Ellie.

The best she could do tonight was help him to switch off for a while. She knew his gaze was on her back as she ran her finger along the books on the shelf, spelling the titles out quietly to herself.

Reaching for the book that she and Izzy had shared, she turned to Jack. 'I don't suppose you'd like to read…'

He grinned. 'I'd be honoured. Will Miss Palmer mind?'

'She'll understand.' What he needed was to let it all go, just for a few hours. And Cass didn't know a better way than this. She handed him the book, settling down next to him on the sofa, and Jack opened it and started to read.

Slowly, they slipped into another world together. The space between them seemed to diminish as they travelled the same paths, thought the same thoughts. And Jack's voice lost the sharp edge of stress that she'd heard in it all evening.

He finished the chapter and they embarked greedily on the next. But it was too much. When they stopped for a while, to talk sleepily, the book slipped from Jack's fingers and Cass caught it before it fell to the floor.

He looked so peaceful. Waking him up would only bring him back to a present that he needed to forget for now if he was going to face it tomorrow. Carefully, Cass manoeuvred Jack round on the sofa, taking off his shoes, disentangling herself from his arms when he reached for her, and fetching the duvet and a pillow from his bed to keep him warm.

Maybe she should make some attempt to slip his jeans off; he'd be more comfortable. She reached under the duvet, finding the button on the waistband and undoing it. Jack stirred, and she snatched her hand away.

*Enough. Go to bed.* Cass left Jack sleeping soundly on the sofa and crept upstairs.

When Jack woke, the feeling of well-being tempered the knowledge that he wasn't where he was supposed to be. He was still in his clothes, but when he moved he realised that the waistband of his jeans had been loosened. He fastened the button again, a little tingle of excitement accompanying the thought that Cass must have undone it, and kicked the duvet off.

Exactly what clinical level of unconsciousness did a man need to attain before he didn't notice the touch of Cass's fingers? Jack dismissed the notion that she must have slipped something into his cocoa and sat up. A loud crash sounded from the kitchen, propelling him to his feet.

'Daddee…' Ellie was sitting at the kitchen table, holding her arms out for her morning kiss. Cass was on her knees, carefully scooping up the remains of a jar of peanut butter, and shot him an embarrassed look.

'Did we wake you?'

'No, he was awake.' Ellie settled the matter authoritatively. 'So we can make some noise if we like.'

Jack chuckled, lifting Ellie from her chair and kissing her. 'Yes, but you still can't make a mess. What do you say to Cass?'

'Sorry. My hand slipped.' Ellie repeated her current excuse for pretty much anything, and Cass got to her feet.

'That's okay, sweetie. There wasn't much left in there.'

'There's another jar in the cupboard.' It didn't look as if

Cass had started her own breakfast yet. 'Thanks for getting Ellie up.'

Cass grinned. 'Call it a joint effort. Ellie picked out what she wanted to wear and I helped with some of the buttons.'

He noticed that Ellie had odd socks on and decided not to mention it. He could rectify that easily enough when he got her into the car.

'I really appreciate it, Cass.' He tried to put everything that he felt into the words. 'Last night, as well…' Last night had helped him face everything a little better this morning.

For a moment her gaze rested on his face, asking all the questions that she couldn't voice with Ellie around. A sudden rush of warmth tugged at his heart, leaving Jack smiling, and she nodded.

'You're going in to see her today?'

'Yes. Shall I give you a call and let you know how she is?' That seemed important somehow. That Cass would be expecting his call.

'I'd really like that.'

Tuesday had brought no change in Mimi's condition, but Wednesday morning brought hopes that she might be woken later on in the day. Cass ate her lunch with her phone in front of her, on the table. When it buzzed, she snatched it up.

'Could I ask an enormous favour?' Jack asked a little awkwardly.

'Sure. Name it.'

'They're waking Mimi up today. Rafe and Charlie, her brother, are with her at the moment, but I'd really like to go in and see her after work.' A short pause. 'There are some things I'd like to tell her.'

'That's really good news. I'll get some shopping on the way home if you like.'

'No… We've got plenty of everything. I was wondering

if you could look after Ellie for a while. It's just that Sarah's going to her evening class tonight…'

Cass swallowed hard. Shopping would have been the easier option, but Jack needed time with Mimi. She could do this. 'Yes, of course. Take your time with Mimi; we'll be fine.' Her voice rang with a confidence she didn't feel.

'Thanks.' He sounded relieved. 'I really appreciate it. Sarah will drop her home on her way to her class…'

She took Sarah's mobile number just in case. Then Cass placed her phone back on the table, wondering what she'd just done.

'Guys…' The ready room was buzzing with activity, and most of her colleagues had children of their own. 'I need some help here. I'm looking after a four-year-old this evening. What am I going to do with her?'

Eamon turned, chuckling. 'Easy. First thing to do is feed her. No sweets or sugary stuff, or she'll be running around all night…'

Pete broke in. 'Find her something she likes on TV for an hour, and then ask her to show you her favourite story book. She'll tell you what it says; they know their favourites by heart.'

Cass laughed, spinning a screwed-up ball of paper at Pete's head. 'I can manage a kid's storybook. Big writing, spaced-out words.'

'There you go then. If in doubt, go for princesses; they're all the rage at the moment,' Eamon added with a laugh. 'Sorted.'

Cass wasn't so sure. A menu and a schedule of activities for the evening was the least of her worries. Looking after Jack's child, in Jack's house, was a mocking counterfeit of all the things she wanted so much but couldn't have. She was just going to have to rise above that and maintain some kind of mental distance.

Tea was accomplished, albeit with the maximum amount of mess. Jack had called, saying that after having slept for the whole afternoon, Mimi was now awake and relatively alert, and Cass told him to stay with her.

Ellie selected her favourite cartoon and Cass sat down on the sofa with her to watch it, while Ellie kept up a running commentary of what was going to happen next.

'The monster's coming...'

'Where?'

'They're going into the forest. He's hiding...' Ellie covered her eyes.

'Hey. It's okay.' Cass assumed that Ellie knew that too, but that didn't seem to erode the tension of the moment for her.

'Cassandra...' Ellie flung her arms around Cass's neck, seeming genuinely terrified, and every instinct demanded that Cass hug her back.

This moment should hurt, but Ellie was just a little girl and it was Cass's name she'd called. Cass felt herself relax, holding Ellie tight. It was just the two of them, and she and Ellie could protect each other from the monsters that lurked in both their heads.

When Jack got home the kitchen was empty, apart from the remains of a meal which looked big enough to feed a whole army of four-year-olds. Upstairs, Ellie was in bed and her room was uncharacteristically tidy. Cass was sitting by her bed, the closed book on her lap indicating that she'd resorted to improvisation for Ellie's bedtime story.

'Daddy...? I had a nice time...' Ellie's voice was sleepy and Jack leaned over, kissing his daughter's forehead.

Cass's face tipped towards him, tenderness shining from her eyes. He nodded in response to her mouthed question about Mimi, and she smiled.

'Do you want to take over?' She was halfway out of the

chair next to Ellie's bed and Jack shook his head. He'd worried about Ellie becoming too reliant on Cass, but in truth it was he who was beginning to feel he couldn't do without her. Ellie was clearly a lot more relaxed about things.

'What's the story about?'

Cass thought. 'Well, there's this princess. Beautiful, of course, and she's got her own castle.'

'Naturally.' Jack sat down on the end of Ellie's bed.

'And she wants her own fire engine…' Ellie woke up enough to show that she'd been following the plot.

'Right. And does she get it?' Jack found himself smiling. Not the tight, forced smile he'd been practising for the last couple of days, but one which came right from the heart.

'Only after she passes her exams and the fitness test.' Cass was clearly intent on making the thing believable.

'And she's going to rescue the prince.' Ellie chimed in.

Jack chuckled. 'Don't let me stop you, then. This I have to hear.'

The soft light from the bedside lamp had transformed Jack's features into that very prince. Handsome and brave. Someone who could fight dragons and somehow turn an impossible situation into a storybook ending. When the princess had finished rescuing him, he rescued her back and everyone lived happily ever after.

When Ellie finally drifted off into sleep neither she nor Jack moved. Holding on to the magic for just a little while longer, despite there being no excuse to do so.

But this was no fairy tale. Jack wasn't hers, any more than Noah or Ellie were. Cass rose quietly from her chair, putting the book back in its place, and walked out of the room, leaving Jack to draw the covers over his sleeping child.

The air in the kitchen was cool on her face. She stacked

the dishwasher and tidied up, then heard a noise at the doorway.

'Oh! You surprised me.' Despite all of her efforts to bring herself back to reality, Jack still looked like a handsome prince. 'How's Mimi?'

He nodded. 'Very drowsy, and a bit incoherent at times, but that's just to be expected. She's doing well. Thanks for looking after Ellie.'

'It's no trouble. How about you—are you okay?'

'I'm fine.' Cass sent him a querying look and he flashed her a smile. 'Really.'

Cass nodded, picking up a cloth and giving the worktop a second wipe. Jack didn't move and the silence weighed down on her, full of all the things they'd left unsaid.

'Would you like a pizza princess? There are some left over in the fridge. They don't actually look too much like princesses...' She was babbling and closed her mouth before anything too crazy escaped.

'I'd like to thank you—for what you said the other night.'

When she turned, the warmth in Jack's eyes seemed more like heat now. Delicious heat.

'I've been re-evaluating. Giving the believing thing a try.'

Something caught in her throat. 'H... How's that going?'

'It's...different.' His gaze dropped to the floor. 'Can I believe in you, Cass?'

She didn't know how to answer that. But it definitely needed an answer. She touched his hand and he gripped hers tight, pulling her towards him.

'I want you to know...' He shook his head as if trying to clear it. 'I didn't ask you here for this.'

'Anything can be re-evaluated.'

For a moment they were both still. As if the next move would be the deciding one, and neither quite trusted themselves to make it.

'I can't promise you anything, Cass. I'm not the man you want…'

He was exactly the man she wanted. No lies, no strings and none of the attendant heartbreak. He was saying all the right things, and making her feel all the right things too.

'Then we're even. I won't promise anything either.'

It was all either of them needed to know. There was no need to hide any more, and the air was electric with whispered kisses.

Then more. Much more, until the kitchen was no longer the place to be and the bedroom was the only place in the world.

They tiptoed up the stairs in an exaggerated game of having to be quiet. Jack looked in on Ellie, closing her bedroom door, and then turned to Cass.

'Asleep?' She allowed her lips to graze his ear.

'Fast asleep.' He led her to his own bedroom and as soon as he'd shut the door behind them, he pulled her close. 'Be quiet, now…'

That wasn't going to be easy. His kiss was just the start of it, and when his hand found her breast Cass swallowed a moan.

'Keep that up and I'll be screaming…' The thought of being in his arms, all the things that he might do, made her want to scream right now.

'No, you won't.' His body moved against hers, his arm around her waist crushing her tight so that she could feel every last bit of the friction. 'You're not going to have breath enough to scream.'

She could believe that. Cass fought to get her arms free of his embrace and pushed him backwards towards the bed. He resisted the momentum, imprisoning her against his strong body. 'Oh, no, you don't…'

Cass relaxed in his arms, letting herself float in his

kisses. Balancing her weight against him, curling her leg slowly around his.

'Oof...' He fell back on to the bed, caught off balance, and she landed on top of him, breaking her own fall with her arms. 'Nice move, princess...'

'I have more.' She pinned him down, running her hand across his chest, luxuriating in the feel of his body. He gasped as her hand found the button on his jeans, and she felt his body jolt as she slipped her fingers past the waistband.

'I just bet you do.' Suddenly she was on her back and Jack had the upper hand again. Holding her down, stretching her arms up over her head, dipping to whisper in her ear.

'I'm going to strip you naked... Then I'm going to find out just how many moves you've got...'

A shard of light from the hallway. Jack froze.

# CHAPTER TWELVE

'DADDY! WHAT ARE you doing?'

The one question he'd never had to even consider an answer for. Jack closed his eyes in disbelief, feeling Cass wriggle out from under him.

'Don't hurt her, Daddy.' He heard Ellie pound into the room and he rolled over on to his back, feeling something soft smack against his legs. Ellie had obviously come armed with her teddy bear.

'It's okay, Ellie. It's all right...' How the hell was he going to explain this one?

'Ellie...' Cass's laughing voice. 'Ellie, it's okay. We were just playing. Daddy was tickling me.' Jack opened his eyes and saw Cass, on her feet and swinging Ellie up in her arms.

'Like this...' Ellie's fingers scrunched against Cass's shoulder in a tickling motion.

'Just like that.' She plumped down on to the bed, rolling Ellie on to her back and tickling her. Cass seemed to have a better handle on the situation than he did. Maybe because she didn't have to worry about surreptitiously refastening any buttons.

'What's the matter, Ellie?' He waited for their laughter to subside, wishing his wits would unscramble themselves.

'I had a bad dream.' Ellie remembered what she was here for and flung herself into his arms. 'Make it go away.'

'Okay.' He held her tight, flashing Cass an apologetic look, but she just grinned. 'Tell me all about it and we'll make it go away.'

It hadn't taken long to comfort Ellie and Jack had suggested that she might like to go back to bed, but she wouldn't budge. So Cass had put an end to the dilemma by getting Ellie to lie down on the bed next to her, with Jack on the other side.

'I'm sorry.' He mouthed the words quietly over the top of Ellie's head, a mix of uncertainty and regret on his face.

'That's okay.' This seemed so right, so natural. Lying on the bed with Jack, his child curled up against her.

'Really?' He stretched out his hand, brushing the side of her face.

'Not quite what I expected.' She whispered the words quietly so as not to disturb Ellie, and Jack dropped a kiss on to his finger and planted it on to her cheek. 'But it's really nice.'

'Could I hold your hand?' His eyes were so tender. When he folded his hand around hers, in the space above Ellie's head, it felt as if a circle of warmth had closed. One which included her. Cass had often wondered what this would feel like, and given up hope of ever knowing.

She had been so afraid of this, terrified of the hurt when she and Jack were torn apart again. But now that didn't seem to matter. It was complete, a thing of itself that couldn't be touched by anything. Tomorrow it would be gone—Jack wasn't hers to keep and neither was Ellie— but even that couldn't spoil tonight.

She stayed awake for as long as she could, knowing that when she slept it would be the beginning of the end. Ellie was sleeping soundly, and when Jack's eyes finally fluttered closed she watched him sleep. If tonight was going to have to last her for the rest of her life, and right now it felt that it could, she didn't want to miss any of it.

It had been almost forty-eight hours since he and Cass had lain down on his bed with Ellie. Thirty-six since he'd woken, stretching over to plant a parting kiss on Cass's fingers while she slept, before picking Ellie up and taking her into her own bedroom to get dressed. Jack had managed to spend one waking hour without thinking about it, largely due to a difficult call at work, although at night he wasn't doing so well. But he couldn't be expected to control his dreams.

He didn't speak about the shock of having Ellie walk in on them, or what had followed, which had somehow been so much more intimate than the night he'd been expecting. Cass said nothing either and their conspiracy of silence seemed to protect those few short hours from the indignity of careless words or doubts. Jack knew two things for sure. It had been perfect, and it mustn't happen again.

Then a girls' night out put all his resolve to the test. Cass had mentioned that she was going out on Friday night and so Jack and Ellie were on their own for supper. But when she came downstairs, fresh from the shower, her handbag slung over her shoulder and her car keys in her hand, what had seemed just difficult was suddenly practically impossible.

'Where are you off to?' He tried to keep the question casual but he heard a note of possessiveness in his voice. He was going to have to practise that and do better when Ellie was old enough to pick up *her* car keys and go out for the night.

'One of the wine bars in town. The one in Abbey Street.'

He knew the one. Quiet and comfortable, a good place to talk and a nice bar menu.

'Great. Well…' He suppressed the temptation to ask her what time she'd be home.

She glanced into the mirror in the hall, running her fingers through the burnished copper of her hair. The arrangement seemed somehow softer, brushed to lie heavy on her brow, and Jack could see sparkles of twisted silver hanging from her ears. Her lips were… Jack wasn't sure what shade of red that was. Delicious Red, maybe. Kissable Red.

'You look pretty.' Ellie supplied the words that he couldn't. She looked gorgeous. Boots, a black suede skirt and a sheer top with a sleeveless slip underneath, which allowed a tantalising glimpse of the curve of her shoulders and the shape of her arms.

'Thank you, sweetie.'

'I want a handbag like yours.'

'You like it?' Cass flushed a little at the compliment and Jack almost fainted. Was she actually trying to make him dizzy or did she really not know just how amazing she looked?

'I like the dangles…' Ellie ran up to her, tugging at the long fringe that hung from the sides of her bag. Jack imagined that when she walked it mimicked some of the graceful sway of her hips.

'Let Cass go, sweetie.' Ellie was about to throw her arms around Cass and the thought of rumpling such perfection was unbearable. 'She'll be late.'

'Bye, Ellie.' She bent down and gave the little girl a hug, somehow managing to keep her make-up intact and her hair just so. 'See you in the morning.'

'Yeah. Have a good evening.' Jack wondered whether he was going to wait up for her, and decided that if he did so it would be from the safety of his bedroom. Probably with most of the furniture piled up against the door, to at least provide some pause for thought before he marched out to ask her what kind of time she called this and then dragged her into his arms.

'Thanks.' She grabbed her coat, giving a little wave and a bright grin, and Ellie followed her to the front door, which gave Jack the chance to watch Cass walk down the front path and appreciate the fluid movement of her body.

Then she got into her car, a bright pearl shining in a sea of blue paint, mud and rust spots. Jack watched her draw away and turned, taking Ellie back inside. The house seemed suddenly very quiet.

He'd listened to the silence in the living room and then gone to bed early, just to see whether the silence in his bedroom might feel less grating. Finally, at eight minutes past one, Jack had heard the front door close quietly and then the pad of stockinged feet on the stairs.

The soft sound of her bedroom door closing allowed him to track her progress. Jack tried not to imagine her throwing her bag on the bed. Taking off her jewellery and slipping the sheer top from her shoulders. He turned over in bed and resolutely shut his eyes.

The silence seemed less a sign that something was missing and more an indication that all was well. Jack drifted off to sleep, but even then his unconscious mind was unable to filter Cass out of his dreams.

It seemed that Jack's unerring radar for detecting any signs of movement on Ellie's part had failed him once again. Cass, on the other hand, seemed to be picking up that instinct. Despite a late night, she woke early, to the sound of Ellie singing to herself in her bedroom.

She turned over in bed, trying to pretend she hadn't heard. Jack would be up soon and it was his job to look after his daughter. The singing continued, and she found herself out of bed, struggling into her dressing gown, before she had a chance to think about it any further.

'Go back to bed, sweetie...'

Ellie's answering smile indicated that she would do no such thing. She reached her arms up for a good-morning hug, and Cass gave in to the inevitable.

Toast and some juice were followed by coffee for herself and a glass of frothed milk for Ellie. The little girl sat at the kitchen table, carefully mimicking Cass's actions, sipping her milk slowly as if she too felt the caffeine bringing her round after a late night.

'Morning.' Jack was still bleary-eyed, his hair wet from the shower. Suddenly Cass was wide awake.

He looked good enough to eat. His washed-out jeans low on his hips, a dark shirt which seemed to have one of the buttons at the top missing, the extra inch or so of open neckline seeming to draw her gaze. Beautiful. From the top of his head to the tips of his sneakers.

*Stop, it's not like that. I don't even fancy him.* The lies she'd managed to half believe last night were coming back to slap her in the face this morning. And the questions from her friends about who she was staying with and what he was like had suggested possibilities that she'd been doing her best to ignore.

He bent to kiss Ellie and then turned his gaze on to her. 'Did you have a good evening?'

'Yes, thanks. Seems like an age since I've been out.'

He walked over to the kitchen sink, pouring himself a glass of water and downing it in one go. Cass got to her feet.

'I'd better get going. There's bunting to be hung.' She was trying not to notice what she fancied might be the remains of the look she'd seen in his eyes when she'd left the house last night.

'What time does it start, again?'

'Two o'clock.' Cass gave Jack a wide berth, making sure

she didn't accidentally brush against him as she walked out of the kitchen, heading for the shower.

The fire station was decorated with flags and bunting, standing to attention in the stiff breeze, and the two fire engines on the forecourt shone in the sun. Cass looked up at the sky.

'Think it'll rain?'

Mike, another of the firefighters, glanced at the clouds.

'If it does, then it'll add some authenticity to the demonstration.' He chuckled. 'After the last month, I'm not sure I'll be able to get a ladder up unless it's raining.'

'Me too.' Cass tipped her helmet on to the back of her head. 'Shame we don't have bigger puddles out back. We could have done rope and water rescue as part of the demonstration.'

'Don't push it, Cass. Have you seen the roof of the office?'

'No?' She looked across at the prefabricated office, on the far side of the yard.

'Enough water on that flat roof to bath a donkey. I'm surprised it hasn't leaked yet.'

'Suppose we could always take a shot at waterfall rescue.' Cass grinned.

'Is that in the manual? Come on, I bet you know what page.'

'Everything's in the manual. And I wouldn't tell you what page it was on even if I knew; you'd just call me a swot.'

'You're a swot. Everybody knows that.' Mike watched the stream of cars turning into the car park. 'Here they come. Prepare for terror like you've never known before.'

Cass looked for Jack in the sea of heads and saw him with Ellie, who was dressed in red wellingtons and a matching waterproof coat. They were being guided across the yard with the first of the visitors and into the garage, where Mike was overseeing the most important part of the afternoon. The demonstration and being able to see a fire engine up close was the fun bit, but there was a serious message to get across as well.

Everything was distilled down into easy steps that a child might remember if faced with a fire or flood. Cass leaned against the front of the tender, listening to the kids' voices chanting along with Mike's. *Don't hide.* A child's first instinct, to hide away in the face of danger, was every firefighter's worst nightmare.

No nightmares today, though. Cass watched as the station commander's wife made a blood-curdling job of yelling for help from the roof of the garage, and four firefighters raced across the yard with a ladder. She was rescued with the minimum of indignity, as befitted her status, and to general applause. Then some of the smaller kids were lifted up on to a lower platform, where they were held safely by one of the crew until a shorter ladder was run across the yard to perform similar, if less hair-raising, rescues.

In between talking to the first of the groups which clustered around her and showing them around the fire engine, Cass saw Ellie on the platform.

'Help! Fire!' she called across the yard at the top of her voice. The firefighter squatting down next to her said a few words and then grinned as she waved her arms energetically above her head. 'Help! Fire!'

Ellie was duly rescued, received a round of applause and ran back to Jack. He hoisted her up on his shoulders and started to walk towards Cass, coming to a halt behind the family who had just approached her.

She bent towards the two little boys, seeing only Jack. Tall and relaxed, smiling at her.

'What...' She cleared her throat, trying to dislodge the

lump that seemed to have formed. She'd already done this half a dozen times but she was suddenly acutely aware of being watched. And acutely mindful of the gentle dark eyes that were doing the watching.

'What have you learned today?' She waited for the boys' answers and then began to show them the fire engine, making a conscious effort not to rush them through. Finally they accepted the colouring sheets and badges that she handed them, along with the fire safety information for their parents, and walked away talking excitedly.

'Nice badges.' His lips were curved in a quiet smile. That smile of his should be X-rated.

'Sorry. Only for the under tens.' She dragged her gaze away from his and felt in her pocket. 'Which one would you like, Ellie? I've got a pink one here.'

Ellie nodded vigorously and Cass reached up, slipping the badge into her coat pocket. Her arm brushed against Jack's and she pulled it away.

'Would you like to come and see the fire engine, Ellie?'

'You missed a bit.' He lifted Ellie off his shoulders, setting her down on the ground, and leaned towards Cass, mouthing the words to her. *What about the message?*

'Ah. Yes.' This would be a great deal easier if he wasn't so distracting. Was it really legal to be so downright sexy, in public and in the presence of children?

'Ellie, what do you do if there's a fire?' She repeated the words numbly, wondering exactly why it was that suddenly all she could think about was Jack's touch. If she knew the answer, then that would at least be a first step to doing something about it.

'Don't hide.'

'Good. Well done.'

Jack nodded. 'And what else?' Cass frowned at him. He was pinching *her* lines now.

'You shout *Fire!* or *Help!*' Ellie decided to enlarge on

the instructions. 'As loud as you can. And you could wave if you liked.'

'Yes. Waving's good too. You have to make sure that someone sees you and knows you're there.'

'Would you like to see the fire engine, Ellie?' Jack smiled down at his daughter.

'Do you mind? This is all very carefully worked out; I can't have parents stealing my lines.' Cass glared at him and he shot back a mouthwatering look, half-humour, half-remorse, and wholly delicious.

'Sorry. Carry on, I'll just watch.'

'Thank you.' Cass caught Ellie's hand, walking her over to the vehicle.

Jack watched as Cass showed Ellie the fire engine. Then stepped forward when Cass climbed up into the driver's seat, to hand Ellie up to sit with her.

She seemed to light up around children. She was a little awkward with them, in the way that he'd been before he'd had his own child, but she obviously loved their company. Why she'd made the decision to concentrate solely on her career, a marriage to her job which couldn't give her what she so clearly wanted, was just another of the imponderables about Cass.

Jack waited, handing up his phone for a few pictures of Ellie at the driver's wheel and then taking it back for a couple of Ellie waving out of the window at him. Then one of Cass and Ellie, hugged up tight together.

Then Ellie got down, accepting the colouring sheets and running back to him, waving the fire safety instructions that Cass had given her. There was nothing in there he didn't know and practise already; Jack had seen too many burns victims to be anything other than rigorous about fire safety in his own home. But it would be a good exercise to read them through with Ellie, and for them to go round and double-check together.

The next group of children was heading towards them and it was time for him to move on now. He'd hoped that the feeling of tearing himself away from Cass each time they parted might lose its sting, but it never seemed to.

'We're…um…we're all going for a drink afterwards. Friends and families—we're going to a place just out of town with a kids' playroom. If you and Ellie…' She left the sentence unfinished.

'Thanks, but Ellie's been invited to tea with one of her friends. I'm going to take the opportunity to pop in and see Mimi.'

'Yes, of course.'

'Next time, maybe…' This was crazy. Even here, now, he couldn't quite let go. Not while there was still some glimmer in her eyes which told him that Cass had been thinking about how close they'd come to being lovers.

'Yeah. See you later, then.' One short moment of connection, in which Jack fancied that they both shared an understanding of how hard this was. Then he took Ellie's hand, listening to her excited chatter as he walked away.

# CHAPTER THIRTEEN

CASS SAW JACK'S car ahead of hers on the main road and flashed her headlights as he turned into the road that led to his house. His hazard lights winked on and then off again, and his car came to a halt outside the driveway. Cass drew level with him, winding down the window as he leaned across.

'You're early...'

'Yeah.' Cass had nursed a glass of orange juice for half an hour, then decided to go home. And then she'd driven back here. She wasn't quite sure when she'd started thinking of Jack's house as home, but she supposed it must have something to do with looking forward to being there every evening.

She leaned round and saw that the child's seat in the back of Jack's car was empty. 'Where's Ellie?'

'Her friend's mum asked if she'd like to stay for a sleepover. And when I went in to see Mimi she just about managed a hello and then fell asleep.'

'Ah. So you've been deserted.'

He chuckled. 'Yeah. No one seems to want me tonight.'

Not true. And from the look on his face he knew it. She should go. Pretend she'd forgotten her purse and had just popped back from the pub to collect it. Then come back later, when Jack was asleep and the coast was clear.

'Ladies first...' He gestured towards the driveway.

'No, you go.' Probably best to leave a getaway option, just in case. Cass watched as he turned into the hardstanding in front of the house. When she followed suit, she took the turn a little too wide and a bit too fast and jammed her foot on the brake, feeling her front bumper touch something as she came to a halt.

She was shaking as she climbed out of the car, leaving the headlights on so that she could see whether there was any damage to the back of Jack's. A piece of mud had fallen from the front of hers and on to his back bumper and she brushed it away.

'It's okay... I hardly touched you.'

'Yeah? Too bad.' He was facing her, not even glancing at the back of his car. 'Do you want to give it another try?'

'I wouldn't want to dent your bodywork.' Suddenly this wasn't about cars. Cass turned away from him with an effort, reaching for the switch on the dashboard to kill her headlights. When she looked up again he was gone, the front door open and the light in the hall beckoning her.

He was standing in the hallway, leaning against the sturdy newel post at the bottom of the stairs. Waiting for her. Cass stepped inside, letting the door drift to behind her, and Jack smiled.

'So... You think you can put a dent in my bodywork, do you?'

The house was quiet. No need to keep their voices down either, because Ellie wasn't asleep upstairs. Jack seemed to fill the space completely.

'I can't say. Not without a more thorough examination.' She wanted to touch him so badly. Blind to anything else but Jack, because there *was* nothing else.

'You can be as thorough as you like. Since we have a little unexpected time on our hands...' His eyes held all the promise of everything they might just dare to do.

Jack walked towards her. Cass dropped her handbag, hearing her car keys spill out on to the floor as she pulled him close.

The kiss left them both breathless. No amount of air would be enough right now. No amount of that delicious feeling when his fingers brushed her face.

'Jack…' There was nothing left to say. They'd tried to keep their hands off each other and they'd failed. But at least they'd both failed together, and they both knew the terms of their failure.

'I can't do it, Cass… Can't pretend I don't want you.'

'Tonight you don't have to.'

He pulled the zip of her jacket open. No hesitation, but no rush either. She could feel his hunger as he kissed her.

His gaze never left hers as he reached behind her, pushing the front door fully closed. Cass heard the lock engage with a satisfying click and a little thrill of excitement ran through her veins. Locked in with Jack, and a whole house as their playground for the night.

He wrapped his arms around her shoulders, backing her into the sitting room and then settling her against him. 'Alone…'

Cass sighed. 'At last.'

Nothing short of an earthquake could stop them now. Cass could rescue him if the fire of their lovemaking got out of control, and he'd resuscitate her if she happened to pass out. They'd save each other from an impossibly long night spent alone.

Jack smothered the impulse to lead her straight upstairs and get them both out of their clothes as quickly as possible. The ultimate luxury had just dropped unexpectedly into their laps and they had time. Enough time to show her that it wasn't just sex he wanted, but a seduction.

'Light the fire.' Her lips curved. She knew just what he

wanted. The thought of their limbs entwined in the fire-light made him tremble but somehow the match sparked first time and he dropped it on to the kindling, which flared suddenly, licking around the coals stacked above it.

Each time he kissed her it felt new, different, like a first kiss. Jack helped her out of her coat and took his off, slinging them both on to an armchair.

'You are the most stunning woman I've ever seen. When I first opened my eyes and saw you, I thought that the heavens had opened up and you'd flown down to save me.'

She tapped her finger on his chest in laughing reproof. 'You should see someone about that. Want me to call an ambulance?'

'I think I'm beyond help.' He caressed the side of her face. 'My very own personal goddess…'

Cass giggled. '*Your* personal goddess? How possessive is that?'

He leaned in, whispering against her neck. 'Got a problem with it?'

'No, I don't think so. But if I'm a goddess, then perhaps you should kneel.'

The way she bought into his fantasies was the ultimate thrill. 'I can do that.'

'Naked…'

'I can do that too.' He nipped at her ear and she shivered, her thrill of pleasure echoing in his own chest. 'Keep that thought for later, eh?'

'Why? Going anywhere?'

'No. But we need to talk about…to agree on…some means of contraception.' The words sounded unexpectedly hard and unromantic, but that couldn't be helped. The wild, reckless days when *It's all dealt with* was enough to reassure him were gone. He'd changed. Even though neither of them wanted a permanent relationship, he could still care about her and while she was with him he'd keep her safe.

She flushed. Something seemed to stop her in her tracks. 'We do?'

'We can't just leave things to chance, Cass. That's a stupid risk.'

'I wasn't suggesting that... But... Can't you just...do something?'

He wasn't exactly sure what she meant. But a prickle of alarm was working its way round the back of Jack's neck.

'It's a choice we need to make together, isn't it?'

'Yes, of course... It's just... But...' She seemed suddenly desperate. As if he'd just suggested something impossible. 'Whatever, Jack.'

He wasn't prepared for the sudden confusion which ate away at his desire and for the wounded look in Cass's eyes. She seemed determined not to talk about it and the thought occurred to Jack that she was hiding something. If she wanted him to trust her, that wasn't the way to do it.

'I don't understand, Cass. Help me out...' One last plea, in the hope that maybe she would open up. But she seemed to be shrinking away from him with every passing moment.

'Fine. Have it your way.' He turned suddenly, choked by the sour dregs of desire. Walking from the room, he heard the door slam behind him.

# CHAPTER FOURTEEN

Cass dropped to her knees, staring into the fire, hugging her arms across her stomach. She hadn't meant to react like that. Why hadn't she just smiled and forced herself to have that conversation. It wasn't as if Jack had suggested anything outrageous. Of course they needed protection.

But to her ears, speaking about it so bluntly had sounded like a contract, some kind of business proposal. And all of the agony of the past, all her feelings of failure, had come flooding back. Even talking about protection, or the lack of it, brought back memories of the bitterness that had pervaded her old relationship. Memories of the months that she hadn't fallen pregnant ever since they had decided to do away with contraception and try for a baby. Thinking about the possibilities and consequences of sex each and every time. Making it a transaction instead of something sweet.

There had been no interruptions, nothing else to blame, and still they'd fallen at the first hurdle. A kiss, a touch, and then they'd torn themselves apart. They couldn't even manage a one-night stand.

There was no way she could stay here now. She was going to have to suffer the humiliation of turning up on a friend's doorstep and begging a bed for the night. She'd heard Jack go upstairs and the house was silent now. Cass opened the door, tiptoeing up the stairs. If she could leave without having to face him again and see that coldness in his eyes, all the better.

She quickly stuffed her clothes into her bag. Her toiletries were in the bathroom but getting them seemed like too much of a risk, and she could replace them. Zipping her jacket up, she picked up her bag and opened the bedroom door.

All clear. Wherever Jack was, he wasn't going to stop her. It was almost a disappointment, but then what would she do if he did try? Neither of them had said anything too hurtful yet, and it was best she got out of here before they had that opportunity.

She walked quietly downstairs. The hall light had been switched off and she put her bag down, scanning the floor for her car keys.

'Looking for something?' She looked up and saw Jack in the sitting room doorway.

'Car keys.' Keep it short and relatively sweet. Maybe he wouldn't see that she had been crying.

He held something up and Cass saw her key fob dangling from his fingers. She stretched her hand towards it and he snatched his arm away, tucking the keys into his pocket.

Cass swallowed hard. The urge to charge at him, knock him off his feet and grab her keys wasn't productive. Anyway, it probably wouldn't work. 'Can I have my car keys? Please.'

'Yeah. In a minute.' He turned and walked into the sitting room. It seemed she had a choice. Either thumb a lift or break into her own car and hotwire it.

Or she could follow Jack. She'd have to be insane to do that now. It was no particular comfort to know that she could remind herself afterwards that she'd known this was a bad idea and she'd done it anyway.

He was sitting in one of the armchairs, his dark eyes following her every move. Jack waved her towards the sofa and like an automaton, programmed to respond to his every command, she sat down.

'I overreacted, Cass. I'm sorry.'

'That's okay. My car keys...'

'In a minute. Hear me out first.'

'It doesn't really matter, Jack.'

'It does to me. Look, it never much occurred to me to ask what went wrong with any of my relationships. It didn't matter—they were never going to last and it was better just to paper over the cracks and part friends. I made that mistake with Sal too, and now I'll never really know what was going on in her head when she left Ellie with me.'

'This has got nothing to do with you and Sal. You can't use me to put the past right.'

'No. But I can learn from my mistakes.'

Cass sighed. 'Look, the best thing we can do now is to forget about tonight and decide to go our separate ways. As friends...'

'And friends don't talk to each other?' He let the thought sink in for a moment. 'I know I was blunt, and I apologise for that. But I was just terrified of leaving anything to chance, giving history a chance to repeat itself. Surely you can understand that?'

'Yes, of course.'

'You want to say anything?'

'I... No.'

He got suddenly to his feet, frustration leaking from every gesture. Cass thought he was going to throw her keys at her and storm out again, but he grabbed her arms, pulling her to her feet.

'Damn, Cass.' He was clearly in the grip of some powerful emotion that he was struggling to control. 'We were going to sleep together. Is it so difficult to trust me?'

'That's just what I wanted to do, Jack. Trust you and sleep with you. Not have to go through some kind of soulless agreement. I've got enough memories of that to last a lifetime.'

'What do you mean?' Jack was clearly not about to give up.

'I tried for a baby with my ex. Didn't happen.' The coldness she heard in her voice was her only defence. 'He left me, and I don't much blame him. All the charts and the dates, working out when we were supposed to have sex... It turned into a chore and I just used to close my eyes and get it over with. And then, afterwards, when I didn't...' She paused. 'Well, when you stopped things and starting talking about...what we needed to do, it brought back bad memories. I couldn't do it. I didn't want it to be like that with you.'

For a moment Jack seemed paralysed, shock registering on his face. Then he pulled her into a tight hug. 'I'm so sorry, Cass.'

'Don't be.' She held herself stiff and unyielding in his arms.

'You want to argue about *that* as well?'

Suddenly all the fight went out of her. He must have felt it because he sat her back down on the sofa, his arms still around her.

'Can I ask you something?'

'Whatever you like.' It didn't much matter now.

'Did you go to the doctor?'

'Yes. He couldn't find anything wrong with either of us. But there was something—we tried for nearly two years, and it must have been my fault because Paul... He left me because he'd made another woman pregnant.'

He wiped his hand across his face, uttering a soft curse. 'Cass, I'm so sorry that happened to you. But there's no blame attached to this. And sometimes the cause is to do with both partners...'

'Don't try to make me feel better, Jack. Paul has a child. It must be me.'

'Not necessarily. It could have been a combination of factors, some to do with you and some with him. Didn't the doctor explain all this?'

'He gave me some leaflets but I was so stressed out about it all…' The words had seemed to mock her, performing a *danse macabre* on the paper.

'And you didn't ask for help, either?'

'No. I didn't want to admit it to anyone.' The secret had driven a wedge between Cass and the people she was closest to. 'You know what some people in the village say about Miss Palmer? They say *"Poor Miss Palmer"* because she never had children.'

'Really? I'm not sure that's something it would ever occur to me to say. Miss Palmer's a force to be reckoned with.'

'I think so too. I want to be like her…'

'The best at your job? Terrifying? I think you've got that taped…' Jack chuckled as she elbowed him in the ribs, and somehow Cass found herself smiling. The secret was out but it hadn't turned on her like some wild beast. Jack had kept her safe.

He *had* trusted her. He *had* believed in her. It had given him the strength to be sure that there must be a reason for Cass's attitude, and when she'd shared her fears with him he'd understood that reason. The suffocating weight of his own childhood and his concerns for Ellie had seemed to lift, as if naming their fears could somehow allow them to put them aside for a while.

'Do you think… That I could go back and start again?'

'Right to the beginning?' Jack had often wondered the same himself. What it would be like if he could rewind and do it all again, knowing what he knew now. 'I don't think that's possible.'

'Just a week or so.'

That was a bit more attainable. 'Can we leave the part where I'm almost drowned out?'

'Yeah. No getting wet.'

'And I doubt that Ben's all that ready for a repeat of the mud incident either.'

Cass laughed. 'No. I don't imagine he is.'

Jack pulled her close, and when she tipped her face up towards him he dropped a kiss on to her cheek. 'Here?'

'That would be a really good place to start.' He felt her lips move against his skin and suddenly he was right back in the place he'd been an hour ago. With a second chance.

'You keep your eyes open when you're with me, though. I promise you that I'll take care of you and keep us both safe, but you have to let me know that it's me you see. Nothing else.'

'I see you, Jack. Not enough of you at the moment...' She tugged at his sweater and he chuckled.

'Hold that thought. I'll be back in a minute. Less, if at all possible.'

'I'll be waiting.'


Jack fetched a quilt from the cupboard upstairs to spread out in front of the fire, concealing the condoms in its folds.

She sat, watching his every move, the flickering light playing across her smile. When she stood, reaching for him, Jack shook his head and pulled his sweater off.

'Not yet. There's something I want to do for you...'

Her gaze didn't leave his face as he pulled off his clothes. Then he fell to one knee in front of her.

He wasn't prepared for this. Jack had worked hard enough to be confident about his body, but the effect of kneeling before her, naked as the day he was born and of-fering himself to Cass, was extraordinary. When her smile told him that she liked what she saw, he felt his limbs begin to tremble. She ran one finger over his deltoid muscle and Jack felt his shoulders flex in response.

'Look carefully.' Her gaze was running across his skin like electricity and he didn't want this to end any time soon.

She shot him a smile, targeting his chest next, and then his abs. Then she moved behind him and Jack caught his breath as he felt her warm hands on his back. Cass leaned over, bending to brush her lips against his ear and he groaned.

'Very nice. Exceptional, in fact.'

His heart thumped in his chest as she circled him again, stopping to face him. He caught her hand, kissing her fingers. 'All at your service.'

'That I like. Very much.'

'I'll take good care of you, Cass.' He wanted her to know that. Wanted beyond anything for her to believe it.

'I know.' She pulled her sweater over her head and Jack instinctively dropped his gaze to the ground. He'd never much thought about the seductive quality of listening to a woman undress, but this was beyond anything he could have dreamed. The soft scrape of material against skin. When he heard her unzip her jeans, his head began to swim and he gasped for breath.

'Jack...' Her fingers stroked his jaw and he raised his head. The picture of Cass, standing in front of him, naked, proud and strong, her red hair gleaming in the firelight, burned itself into his consciousness like a brand. Jack knew he would never forget this moment.

He was beautiful. Shadows contoured the honed muscles of his shoulders, slipping downwards towards slim hips and strong thighs. Like a fine sculpture of a man, every inch of which had been fashioned by a master craftsman, in perfect form and proportion.

A man less confident about his body might have objected

to this. But Jack's strength allowed them to go places she'd never been before. Allowed them to act out the fantasy without the possibility of bruising his ego.

He wasn't just some abstract being, though. This gorgeous body would be nothing without Jack's warm eyes. The tenderness of his touch as he reached out, sliding his fingers along her curves.

'You are exquisite.' His hands moved to her waist and he drew her in, kissing her hip. Cass's legs began to shake and then gave way altogether, and his grip tightened, holding her as she fell to her knees. Then he pulled her against him in a movement of unashamed power.

Her gaze met his and he kissed her. The ache of wanting him so much was almost unbearable now and she clung to his neck as he picked her up, a tangle of trembling limbs, and laid her down in front of the fire.

Settling himself over her, one arm curled around her back, the other hand moving towards her breast. A bright shiver of anticipation and suddenly Jack stilled, his fingers just a moment away from her skin. Before he'd even touched her nipple it was tight and hard.

Just a breath, a brush of his lips, and then he turned his face up to her. 'Crazy for me?'

'You know I am, Jack.'

'Yeah. I'm crazy for you too, princess.' His hand trailed down, caressing, learning her body. Each time she caught her breath his fingers responded, lingering a little until he tore a cry from her lips. Caught in his gaze, she could hide nothing from him.

Jack didn't know how much more of this he could stand. He felt as if he was melting. So very hard, and so very soft, both at the same time.

She tightened the muscles which cradled him inside her and he gasped.

'You like that…?'

'Yes would be an understatement. Do it again.'

'Your wish…' She did it again, grinning as he cried out. 'Is my command.'

'And yours…' He cupped her breast, stroking the nipple with his thumb, and felt her jolt against him. 'Is mine.'

They'd tested each other and broken every limit that Jack thought he had. Balanced together on the edge of a precipice, one false move would send them over the edge. Jack staved off the inevitable for as long as he could.

His sweet Cassandra. The words echoed in his head for a moment as he saw her break, coming apart at the seams so completely that she took him with her. And, when he came, the sudden violence of each sensation robbed Jack of everything. He belonged to her now.

They rested a little, grinning breathlessly at the racing beat of each other's hearts. Jack folded her in his arms and they lay staring into each other's eyes.

It was still early, though, and they both knew that this wasn't even close to being over. A murmured conversation, stretching like cats in front of the fire. A bottle of chilled Prosecco from the kitchen, which popped satisfyingly, the cork hitting the ceiling. A book, chosen at random from the shelf, which turned out to be a collection of short mystery stories.

He propped the book on her hip, their limbs tangled together. He loved this simple pleasure. Reading to her in front of the fire, feeling her intent gaze.

'Had enough?' Jack got to the denouement of the first story and she moved, sending the book slithering to the floor.

'Not nearly enough.' She picked up his glass, holding it to his lips, and he took a sip. Then she ran the cool rim across the heated skin of his chest.

'Hey… Two can play at that game…' He grabbed the glass from her, touching it to her lips and then her nipple and she yelped, laughing. And then everything else was forgotten as he rolled on to his back, pulling her astride him.

'How many times…' She leaned down to kiss him and he cupped her breasts in his hands. 'How many times can you do it in one night?'

An hour ago, Jack would have said that he wasn't going to be able to move for at least another two days. But Cass had a way of confounding every expectation. 'I have no idea.'

She shook her head in smiling reproof. 'Everyone should know that.'

'Yeah. I guess everyone should.'

No one should have that kind of stamina. The man should come with a warning, stamped across his forehead. *Danger. You will be putty in my hands.* By the time Jack tipped them both out of bed and into the shower, late the following morning, he'd pushed her to her breaking point. Then past it, into a rose-tinted world that seemed to revolve entirely around his smile.

Cass started on Sunday lunch while Jack went to pick Ellie up. That afternoon he set about hanging wind chimes in the little girl's room, positioned so that they sounded every time the door opened. Ellie loved them, and Jack's grin made it quite clear that the loud jangling sound wasn't intended solely to amuse his daughter.

He didn't need to ask whether she would come to him that night, and Cass didn't need to answer. He was waiting, his eyes following her every move as she walked towards the bed. Jack's hand trembled as he pushed the silk wrap slowly from her shoulders.

During the day they never spoke of it, even when they were alone, and hardly even touched. Jack was a friend who had offered her a place to stay while her house was flooded. When darkness fell and the house was quiet, he was her lover. It was simple, intoxicating and they both knew that this relationship, with its split personality, couldn't last.

But for two weeks it did. A secret from everyone. Untouched by the past, because they both knew that there was to be no future to it.

## CHAPTER FIFTEEN

'WAKE UP. WAKE UP...' Jack whispered into her ear, jerking the coffee out of Cass's way as she suddenly sat bolt upright in bed. That hadn't been quite the reaction he was looking for, but he'd watched her eyes flutter slowly open once already this morning.

'Uh... What's the time?'

'Eight-thirty.' She looked gorgeous when she woke. Particularly like this, the bedclothes slipping down to her waist, her hair in disarray.

'What?' Jack reared backwards as she shot out of the bed, affording him an even better view. Then she stilled. 'It's Saturday, isn't it.'

'Yeah.' He smiled. 'Coffee?'

She took the mug from his hand and took a sip. Then another thought occurred to her. 'Where's Ellie?'

'Downstairs. I heard her get up about an hour ago. I told her you were probably sleeping and not to come up here and disturb you.' Cass was up before Ellie during the week, and at weekends the wind chimes gave Jack a chance to head her off before she came into his bedroom. It had worked so far.

She took another gulp of coffee. 'I should be getting going.'

'Not without us, you're not.' Martin had called last night

to say that the flood water had receded from around Cass's house. He wasn't letting her go back there alone a second time.

'But I said—'

'Yeah. I said too.'

'Thought you might have forgotten that.' She pushed his legs a little further apart with her foot so she could perch on his knee. Jack took the cup from her hand, taking a sip.

'Post-coital memory loss isn't permanent. I'm coming to help. Whether you like it or not.'

'Too bad.' She took the cup back, raising it to her lips. 'It'll be cold and wet…'

'Are you even listening to me?'

She leaned forward, brushing a kiss on his brow. 'Yes, I'm listening. I'm just not sure how I'll feel about it all.'

'Then let me feel it with you. Whatever it is.' Jack stood up, tipping her off his knee and kissing her cheek. 'Get dressed.'

They were on the road by nine o'clock. The water had begun to drain away from the motorway and it was possible to take Cass's SUV across, Jack walking ahead to check the surface of the road for potholes while Ellie stared out of the window at the water swirling around the wheels. They drove up to the vicarage first to see Sue and Martin, and found Miss Palmer, drinking tea in the kitchen.

'I happened to pop in.' She addressed Cass, giving Jack a smile. 'Is this Ellie?'

Ellie clung to the bottom of Jack's jacket, trying to slide behind his legs. Miss Palmer smiled at her then bent to draw what looked like a large bundle of green felt out of a carrier bag at her feet. 'I can't get this quite right, you know. Oops.'

Something fell to the ground at her feet. Ellie peered at it then stepped forward to pick it up. 'Ah, thank you, dear.'

Miss Palmer took the plastic toy away from her and put it on the table.

'It's a dinosaur…'

'Yes, dear. I've got some more here somewhere.' Miss Palmer fiddled with the bundle of felt and another plastic dinosaur fell out. 'Ah, there it is.'

Ellie's shyness was no match for Miss Palmer and the little girl was hooked. She climbed up on to a chair next to Miss Palmer, craning across to see what she was doing. Sue went out into the hallway, calling up the stairs, 'Hey, you two. Dinosaur Park…'

Jack raised a questioning eyebrow in Cass's direction. 'Bit of a tradition around here. I used to love Dinosaur Park.'

By the time they'd drunk their tea, the felt had been rolled out on the table to display an impressive land-scape—grass, rivers and desert—all sewn in a patchwork of colours. Ellie was wide-eyed, clutching a surprisingly life-like volcano made out of fabric, and Sue's children were carefully arranging a waterfall made out of sparkly thread, which came complete with a pool at the bottom. Miss Palmer was talking to them quietly, lining up plastic trees and a variety of prehistoric creatures on the table, ready to complete the scene.

'She can stay here if she wants.' Sue nodded towards Ellie. 'I doubt they'll be finished before lunchtime, and then there's the battle to do.'

'Battle?'

'Yeah.' Cass grinned. 'Don't you know anything about dinosaurs?'

Ellie had to be prompted to give him a hug and a kiss goodbye and turned back immediately to the task in hand. Jack followed Cass down the steep path that led to her house.

She was quiet, seeming to be preparing herself for what was ahead of them. Walking with her head down, across the mud which led to her house. Jack followed, wondering when she was going to stop and take a look around at the damage.

Clearly not until she got inside. The front door didn't move when she tried to push it open and Jack put his shoulder to it. It slowly opened, scraping across the carpet and making an arc in the sticky mud which covered the floor. A foul smell of damp and decay hit them.

This was worse than she'd thought. She'd expected the mud everywhere, the damp and the disgusting smell. Known that the plaster would be bulging and waterlogged, and that there would be brown watermarks on the walls.

And she'd known that it would be upsetting, but Cass hadn't prepared herself for feeling physically sick. She routinely saw a lot worse—homes that had been burned out or flooded. She hadn't lost her home and neither had she lost most of her possessions, as so many had. It was just a bit wet.

She produced a notepad from her pocket. 'Front door.' She wrote the words carefully, the first on a list that was undoubtedly going to get very long. But she was doing okay. She was getting a grip.

Jack followed her in silence as she walked through the hall, stopping to write things down as she went. In the kitchen it was the same story—mud, watermarks on all the floor cupboards and the same horrible smell. Cass had disconnected the cooker unit and propped it up on the worktop, but the unit which housed it was ruined, the particle board swollen and blown.

'Not so bad.' She tapped the floor tiles with the toe of her boot. 'I wonder if I can salvage these and re-lay them.'

'Cass…'

Not now. Not here. If he was too supportive, then she'd just want to cry. Then he'd hug her, and that wouldn't do because they'd agreed that the pleasures of the night shouldn't leak into the day.

She turned abruptly, marching back into the hall and through to the sitting room. Forming most of the large extension at the back of the house, it was usually a great place to sit and relax—large patio windows which looked out on to the river and the trees beyond it. Now it was ruined. The empty bookshelves and TV cabinet were practically falling apart and the same oozing mud disfigured the carpets and walls.

She tasted bile at the back of her throat. Retching and crying, Cass made a run for the kitchen, wrenching open the back door.

'Don't touch me!' She was bent over, the fresh air stinging her wet cheeks, and Cass felt Jack's hand on her shoulder. She heaved in a couple of breaths, beginning to feel a little better.

When she straightened up again, she saw him standing by the back door. 'Sorry about that. Must be the smell. Turned my stomach.'

'Yeah. Must be.' He was watching her intently.

'I'll…get some water from the car.' She walked past him into the kitchen, wondering what Jack was thinking of her.

'Cass.' His voice behind her. 'What we have. It's only nights, right?'

She froze. Cass had known it was a mistake to let him come here. Talking about it was sure to mess everything up. 'Yes…'

'I want one day too. Now… Today…' When she turned, his eyes were dark, with the same intensity she saw in them every night. Jack walked slowly towards her and wrapped her in a hug.

Without any warning at all, she started to cry. Big choking sobs, while she clung to his jacket. Jack soothed her, kissing the top of her head, holding her tight.

She'd cried for a long time. Blown her nose and cried a bit more. Jack had fetched water for her from the car, along with the flask of hot tea, and they'd sat on the kitchen doorstep together, sharing a cup of tea. Despite the devastation around them, Jack was beginning to feel that he could get used to this daytime thing.

Someone banged on the door. 'Stay here. I'll get it.' Jack hurried through to the front door, heaving it open.

Martin stood on the doorstep. On the road a small group, mainly men but some women as well, all shod in wellington boots. Jack recognised Ben's parents, his father carrying a couple of shovels to help clear the mud from the floors.

'I know Cass doesn't want any help.' It seemed that Martin had been appointed to take the first crack at persuading her otherwise.

'She's taking any help she can get. Come in.' Jack stood back from the door and Martin beckoned to the group behind him.

*What's going on?* She mouthed the words at him as he entered the sitting room.

'Your friends have come to help you out.'

'They don't need...'

'Yes, actually, they do.' Jack put his arm around her, bundling her through to the hallway, which was filling up quickly.

'Martin...' Tears welled in her eyes again and she clutched hold of Jack's sweater.

'Thanks for coming.' Jack voiced the words for her and Martin gave a small nod.

'Where are we going to start, then?'

\* \* \*

The amount that could be achieved by a dozen people in less than four hours was amazing. The house had been aired through, and mud shovelled into buckets to be carted out. Carpets had been taken up and some of the mud had been scraped from the floorboards. In the kitchen, the cupboards and floor were washed clean and the smell of disinfectant started to permeate the air.

The furniture left in the sitting room was beyond repair, and was dismantled and removed. At two o'clock Martin received a text, and called for everyone to down tools.

'Lunch in the church hall, ladies and gents. Half an hour.'

Cass had slipped from tearful and embarrassed, through red-cheeked and into beaming. Then back to tearful again as she stood at her front door, hugging everyone and thanking them as they filed out of the house.

'I don't know what to say...' She stood in the doorway waving as everyone made their way back along the track to the village.

'I think you said it, didn't you? Anyway, I think this morning was all about what the village wanted to say to you.'

'It was so good of them...'

'What goes around comes around, Cass.'

'Thank you. For today.'

He nodded. 'Do it again tomorrow?'

'No. You spend tomorrow with Ellie, and I'll come here. I feel better about things, seeing how much difference we've made today.'

'All right.' Jack would have a quiet word with Martin and make sure that Cass wasn't alone tomorrow. And maybe she was right. He'd asked for one day and she'd given it, and maybe that was enough for now.

# CHAPTER SIXTEEN

THE WEEK HAD seen them slip back into their easy routine. Jack had been looking forward to the weekend, wondering if perhaps Cass might be persuaded to take some time off from her work at the house, for an outing with him and Ellie. And then, suddenly, nothing else existed. The phone call on Friday afternoon, from a parent of one of the kids from Ellie's class, drove everything else from his head. Just the need to drive, to be there.

He could hear sirens in the distance, and he willed them on. Jack knew they were probably going in the same direction as he was, and if he couldn't reach Ellie then someone had to. Anyone.

He took the turn into the small side road that led to the school and slammed on the brakes, narrowly avoiding a fire engine that was parked up ahead. Getting out of the car, he ran, not stopping to even close the driver's door, let alone lock it.

'Jack…Jack!' He heard a woman's voice and scanned the crowd. 'Jack!' The mother of a little boy in Ellie's reception class ran towards him.

'Hannah.' He caught her hand, then put his arm around her. 'What's happening?'

'All the other kids are out. But the annexe…' Hannah's chest started to heave and Jack willed her to stay calm.

'Sarah told me that part of the building had collapsed.'
Ethan had stayed home today with a bad cold, but Jack had
dropped Ellie off at school this morning.

'Yes. The ground's so wet… The kids' classroom looks
okay from the outside, but they're still in there.'

'Okay. Hannah, they'll get to them. The firefighters
are trained for this; they know exactly what to do…' Jack
wasn't sure whether he was trying to reassure Hannah or
himself.

*Stop. Look around. Assess the situation, then act.* His
own training came to the fore and Jack swallowed down his
panic, the overwhelming need to have Ellie safe in his arms.

A pattern emerged from the chaos. A line of older children were leaving the main entrance of the school, shep-
herded by their teachers towards the sports field, which
was some way from the building. There, children were
being counted and checked, while a small group of parents waited anxiously.

He took Hannah's hand, walking swiftly around the
back of the building, trying to control the feeling that he
just needed to sweep everything in front of him away and
find Ellie. What had once been the school hall was now a
pile of rubble and the two-storey annexe beyond it, which
housed the reception classroom, was completely cut off.

'They got the class on the ground floor out through the
windows.' Hannah was hiccupping the words out through
her tears. 'But Jamie and Ellie were upstairs. I saw her in
the window, Jack.'

Jack looked up at the window, his heart leaping as he saw
a small figure, climbing up on to the low, wide sill. *Ellie.*
She was waving her hands above her head and seemed to
be shouting.

'Ellie…' He roared her name, but in the general activity
she didn't hear. 'Ellie!'

Someone held him back and he struggled free. The firefighters already had ladders up at the windows, and one of them climbed up. Jack saw Ellie walk along the windowsill towards him, reaching through the safety bars to press her hands against the glass.

They seemed to be talking. The firefighter called for quiet and a hush fell on the people below.

'Good girl. We saw you. Get down from the window now, sweetie, and stand over there.' The firefighter pointed into the classroom and Ellie obeyed him.

'Good girl. That's my good girl.' Jack sent the whispered words up into the air, wondering if Ellie knew he was here for her. Praying that she did.

'Why don't they just break the windows?' Hannah had her eyes fixed on the huge picture windows, which looked out on to the rolling countryside beyond.

'Windows that size…if they break them they might hurt the kids.' Jack shivered as he thought of shards of glass raining down on Ellie's head.

'Where's the teacher…?'

Good question. The thought of fifteen four- and five-year-olds alone up there made his blood run cold.

He wrapped his arm around Hannah, hurrying to the cordon of police and teachers which surrounded the scene. 'Let me through. Paramedic.' At the sight of his uniform he was waved through and, taking Hannah with him, he made for the two ambulances, parked next to a fire engine.

'Josie—' he recognised the paramedic who was waiting by one of the ambulances '—what's happening?'

'There's a class of fifteen kids and a teacher, trapped in there. No sign of the teacher, but there's a little girl who keeps coming to the window. There's a fire crew gone in.' Josie pointed towards a pile of rubble which almost filled a gaping hole in the wall. Above it, clean plasterwork with a line of pictures still pinned to it in a parody of normality amongst the destruction.

As he watched, one of the pictures fluttered from the wall on to the ground. A groaning sound, and a chunk of plasterwork flattened it as it detached itself from the wall and crashed down. Hannah let out a little scream of terror.

'Okay, Hannah. It's just a piece of paper…' He tightened his arm around Hannah's shaking shoulders. The image of frailty, crushed and broken, had torn at his heart too.

Josie was shaking her head, her eyes fixed on the classroom windows. 'She didn't hesitate. That woman deserves a medal…'

'What?'

'The firefighter. She saw the little girl and she was the first in, even though there have been great chunks of stuff coming down. Three of the men followed her.'

'Red hair?' A trickle of hope found its way into Jack's heart.

'Dunno, she had a helmet on. I didn't know it was a woman but I heard her call out to someone.'

*Cass. It must be Cass.* 'I'm going in…' Jack let go of Hannah and started to walk, and Josie pulled him back.

'Don't be an idiot.'

'Ellie's in there.'

Josie paled suddenly. 'All the same, Jack. If you get hit on the head by a lump of concrete then that's just another thing they'll have to deal with.'

He didn't care. 'Stay here, Hannah. I'll find them.'

'Jack…' Both Hannah and Josie were pulling at him now, and Jack shook them off. Then he looked up. Two figures had appeared in the window, with dark jackets and yellow helmets. Firefighters.

Cass. She and the other firefighter were making short work of the safety bars across one of the windows, and they opened it wide. Jack wondered where the other two men who had gone in were, and hoped that their absence didn't mean that there were casualties to attend to.

'Jamie…' The children were being lifted out one by one, into the arms of the men on the two ladders which had been raised to the window, and passed down to the ground. Hannah sprinted forward, pushing a policeman who tried to block her path out of the way in a surprising show of strength. She reached her son and fell to her knees, hugging him close.

*Ellie. Where was she? Why wasn't she the first?* Jack looked up at the window and saw Cass, with Ellie in her arms. She was talking to her, waiting for the firefighter on the ladder to be ready to take her, and Ellie was nodding.

Then a kiss. Jack almost choked with emotion as he saw Ellie handed safely from the window and into the arms of the man on the ladder.

Cass's attention was now on the next child, lifting him up and talking to him. But all Jack could see was Ellie. He ran forward and heard her voice as she was carried down the ladder.

'I shouted for help…'

'That's right, sweetie. Well done.' The firefighter was smiling as he climbed down.

'Daddeee! Cassandra rescued me.' Ellie held out her arms to Jack and then he felt her small body against him. He stammered his thanks to the firefighter, who nodded, climbing back up the ladder to fetch the next child.

'Are you all right, honey?' His first instinct was just to hold her, but he forced himself to check Ellie's small body for any signs of blood or injury.

'Cassandra came to find me. I got rescued…' There was clearly nothing wrong with Ellie's lungs.

'That's right, darling.' He looked up and saw Cass pass the next child out of the window. When she'd done so, her gaze scanned the people below her and found Ellie, who waved at her excitedly. Cass's grin told Jack that she'd seen what she had been looking for, and that she knew Ellie was safe.

The children were being marshalled into a group around the ambulances by parents and teachers so that each could be checked over. Jack walked across, holding Ellie tightly against his heart.

He saw Sarah running towards them and Ellie waved to her.

'I was rescued!' Clearly Ellie wanted everyone to know. Sarah flung her arms around them both and Ellie struggled to get out from between their bodies so that she could see what was going on.

The last child was being brought down the ladder and Jack did a swift headcount. Fourteen. He made only fourteen. And where was their teacher? He heard Cass's shout behind him.

'Paramedic...'

Josie looked up and grabbed her bag, making for one of the ladders. Jack reluctantly passed Ellie into Sarah's arms.

'Will you take her?' The words tore at his heart but he knew what he had to do.

'Of course. As soon as she's been checked over, I'll take her back home. I left Ethan with my neighbour so I don't want to be any longer than I can help.' Sarah turned to Ellie. 'Daddy's got to go and help Cassandra. We'll wait for him at home, eh?'

Ellie nodded. 'Are you going to rescue Miss Elliott?'

'Yes, sweetie. I'll be back as soon as I can.' Jack turned and made for the ladders.

It was no surprise that after the first paramedic was helped through the window, Jack appeared right behind her. Both of them had been provided with helmets and jackets.

'Just couldn't stay away, could you?' Cass grimaced at him.

'Nope.' Jack looked around the empty classroom.

Cass nodded. 'Good. Keep the helmet on.'

She led the way across the empty classroom, holding her arm out in front of him to keep him back from the door as she opened it. She heard Jack let out a quiet curse as he looked along the corridor, at the gaping hole in the floor that separated the classroom door from the far end of the corridor. 'How did you get through here?'

'We made it.' It hadn't been easy, and they'd been showered with lumps of loose plaster falling from the ceiling. But when she'd seen Ellie up at the window, Cass had remembered the promise she'd made to the little girl. *'If you go to the window and call for help, the firefighters will rescue you.'* That wasn't the kind of promise you made lightly.

'What's the situation?'

'The teacher's at the bottom of the hole, with the boy. He's lying underneath her and we don't know how badly either of them are hurt yet. There's a team trying to get to her from the back, on ground floor level, but the doorways are blocked with rubble and at the moment the only way is through here. So a second team has been working to get a ladder down to her.'

'Can you get me down there?'

'It's not safe.' The roof was still intact but cables and lumps of ceiling plaster dangled precariously over the hole. The other paramedic had already backed away into the safety of the classroom, and if he was going to stick to protocol then Jack should as well.

'Tell me something I don't know. Get me down there, Cass.'

She nodded. 'Okay. It'll be a minute before we're ready to go down.'

'Is she conscious?'

'We think so. When we came along the corridor we heard her groaning, and when we called down she replied.

There was stuff coming down from the ceiling and she was covering the child with her body.'

'What happened?' Jack's face had formed into a mask of determination.

'I think the boy must have run out of the classroom and the teacher followed him. We found the door locked, and she must have thought to lock it behind her to keep the rest of the kids inside. Somehow, she and the boy both fell.'

He nodded. 'Can we get her up to this level?'

'We could, but it would be better to wait for the team coming in via the ground floor. We'll have to make a decision on that when you've assessed her injuries.' Cass looked up as someone called her name. 'They're ready.'

Jack followed her over to the mouth of the hole and Cass climbed carefully down, flattening herself against the ladder as a shower of dust and debris fell from the ceiling. Picking her way across the rubble, and what looked like the remains of a photocopier, she headed towards the woman.

'Annabel... Annabel, I'm Cass.'

Annabel's eyelids flickered and she moaned. 'Cass...'

'Lie still. Not too long now before we get you out of here.'

'Take him...' Annabel cried out in pain as she shifted slightly and a boy's dirty, frightened face peered out at Cass.

'Okay. Okay, we're going to take you both. Just hang in there.'

The boy started to crawl out from the crevice below Annabel's body. Somehow, even though she was clearly badly injured, she'd managed to get him into the safest place she could, protecting him in the only way that was available to her. Dust and plaster was floating down from above them and Cass crouched over Annabel, sheltering her and the child as best she could.

Jack was making his way towards her with the medical

bag, which had been lowered down after them. As soon as he reached them, Cass let go of the boy, who wriggled free of his hidey-hole and straight into Jack's arms.

The boy was handed back to the firefighter who had followed Jack down, ready to be carried back up to the classroom where the other paramedic was waiting. Cass held her position, sheltering Annabel, while Jack started to check her over, talking quietly to reassure her.

A piece of something hit the back of her helmet and Jack glanced upwards. 'Okay?'

'Yep. Keep going.' Annabel was injured and defenceless. And she'd already shown such bravery. Cass would keep shielding her with her own body for as long as it took.

Jack gave her the briefest of smiles and then turned his attention back to his patient.

'Sweetheart. Annabel… I'm giving you pain relief. It'll kick in pretty quickly.' He murmured the words and Cass saw Annabel nod.

'The children…' She opened her eyes, trying to focus on Jack. 'You're Ellie's dad…'

'Yes, that's right. The children are all safe, thanks to you. And Shaun is okay as well—the firefighters are taking him out of the building.'

'I picked him up and the ground just… My leg…'

'You did just great, Annabel. You protected them all.' Jack's sideways glance at Cass told her that he'd come to the same conclusion she had. Annabel and Shaun must have fallen together and she must have landed awkwardly, trying to protect him.

'So cold. Don't want to…die.' A tear dribbled from the corner of Annabel's eye and Cass shifted her position so that she could take her hand.

'You're not going to die.' Jack brushed the side of her face with his fingers to keep her attention. 'Hey… Annabel.'

'Yeah… Too much paperwork…' Annabel grimaced.

'Far too much. I know you're hurting, but you're going to mend. Just hold on to Cass and we'll be getting you out of here as soon as we can. Got it?' Cass knew exactly what the warmth in Jack's eyes could do. He could make her believe anything, and she hoped that Annabel would believe him now.

'Yes...'

News was passed through that the firefighters, working to get through at ground floor level, were almost there. Jack worked on Annabel quickly and carefully, preparing her to be moved. A neck brace and temporary splints for her legs. A thermal blanket, to try and warm her a little, and an oxygen mask.

Annabel's eyes followed him. Somehow, Jack had managed to become not just someone who could give her medical help but her lifeline. It was almost as if he was keeping her going, just by the sheer force of his personality, that warmth in his eyes. Staving off the shock which made Annabel's hand ice-cold in hers.

The noise of boots clambering over the rubble heralded the arrival of the stretcher. Jack slid a lifting board under her body and Cass helped him transfer her to the stretcher, quickly securing the straps and tucking the thermal blanket around her.

'Okay, sweetheart.' Jack smiled down at Annabel. 'We're on our way.'

# CHAPTER SEVENTEEN

JACK WAITED UNTIL the ambulance had drawn away, carrying Annabel to the hospital. Cass came to stand beside him, watching the vehicle negotiate its way past the fire engines and down the lane.

'Brave woman,' she murmured.

'Yeah. Josie's going to find out how she is when she goes off shift, and call me.'

'Do you think...?' She shrugged. 'How did she seem, to you?'

'Shock. One leg broken, and the other is probably fractured. Cuts, bruises, and she's got a cracked rib and what looks like a broken wrist. I couldn't find anything else, but they'll be checking her over further at the hospital to make sure.'

Cass nodded. 'I hope she's all right. Are you going off shift now?'

'Yes, I want to take Ellie straight home.'

'Okay.' Cass turned towards the fire engine. 'See you later.'

He caught her arm. 'Cass. Thank you.' There was nothing more he could say. When he'd seen Ellie in Cass's arms his heart had almost burst with relief.

'Yeah. Any time.' She grinned up at him and he knew that she understood.

By the time Jack got Ellie home she was starting to ask questions, and to realise that her experience hadn't been just another game. Was her teacher hurt? Why did her school fall down—was their house going to fall down too? He tried to answer everything as honestly as he could without feeding his daughter's fears.

She wanted to hold on to him, and he settled down in front of the TV to watch her favourite film with her. Even that didn't seem to get her singing and dancing around the room, as it usually did.

Cass was a little later than usual and, when he heard the front door close, Ellie didn't get up and run to greet her. When she walked into the sitting room, she was smiling.

'Hey, Ellie.' She squatted down in front of her. 'How are you doing?'

'All right.' Ellie turned her solemn eyes on to Cass without letting go of Jack's shirt.

'I've got something for you.' Cass was holding one hand behind her back.

Ellie craned around, trying to see what it was. 'Sometimes we meet kids who are really, really brave. And we give them a special certificate.'

'Really?' Ellie's eyes widened, and Jack grinned. So that was what she'd been up to.

'Yes.' Cass produced a roll of paper from behind her back, tied with a red ribbon. 'So this is for you.'

Ellie took the paper and Jack pulled open the bow with his free hand and unrolled it on Ellie's lap. Her name was on it in large letters framed with curlicues. He ran his finger under the words.

'*Junior Firefighter...*' he read out loud. 'That's you, Ellie. And, look, everyone from the fire station has signed it.' He pointed to the group of signatures, strewn with kisses and hearts. Cass's name was there too, the writing careful and rounded.

He stopped to wonder for a moment how handwriting could possibly be sexy, and then turned his mind to the image at the bottom.

'And there's the fire engine.' The artwork was clearly downloaded from the Internet, but that wasn't the point. Cass had taken the time to print it off on thick paper, and to get it signed by everyone. And Ellie was proud of herself now, not fretful and worrying.

'Say thank you to Cass.' He turned his face up to her, mouthing the words for himself, wondering if she knew just how heartfelt they were. She smiled at him.

'What's for supper?'

Everything was clearly okay in Cass's world if she was hungry. Jack had come to recognise the signs. 'Pasta. Fifteen minutes. Why don't you take Ellie upstairs and you can find a place on her bedroom wall for the certificate. I'll get a frame for it, eh, Ellie?'

The bumps and bangs from upstairs, along with the sound of Ellie's chatter, indicated that there was rather more going on than just the choosing of a place on the wall. Jack laid the table in the kitchen and took the pasta bake from the oven, leaving it to cool. Curious to see what they were doing, he walked upstairs to fetch them instead of calling them down.

The curtains were drawn in Ellie's bedroom, and Jack's hand hovered over the light switch as he popped his head around the door. Then he saw the makeshift arrangement of sheets, held up with a couple of chairs and some twine, forming a tent at the end of Ellie's bed. The glow of torchlight and the mutter of voices came from inside.

For a moment he was transfixed. So this was what it was like. A family. He remembered playing in a tent in the garden with his dad before everything had been shattered and their home had become just a house where grief had pushed the laughter away.

Suddenly it hurt. That swell of pain, all the regret for things he'd never done with his father. For the first time, Jack wondered whether his father had really wanted to leave them like that. Whether, in those last moments, when death must have seemed inevitable, he had thought of his wife and children.

For a moment the feelings choked him. It had been so much easier to blame his father, to be angry at the choices he'd made. But perhaps he'd just been a dad, after all.

Quietly, he walked into the room. The sudden clatter of wind chimes startled him and Ellie came cannoning out of the makeshift tent, almost knocking it down. Jack hadn't noticed the trip wire at his feet.

'We got you, Daddy…' Ellie wrapped her arms around his leg, clinging on tight.

'Yeah, you got me.' He bent down to tickle her and she wriggled with laughter. Then he put one finger over his lips, assuming a stage whisper. 'Where's Cass?'

'In the tent,' Ellie whispered back, her hand shielding her mouth.

Jack dropped to his knees and followed Ellie. Inside the tent, a line of dolls greeted him, their faces impassive. And Cass, sitting cross-legged and a little nervous, as if she'd just been caught doing something she wasn't strictly meant to.

'Can I come in?' Jack grinned at her.

'Yes. Of course.' She shifted a bit to give him room to get inside the tent and Ellie clambered past him to her own spot, next to the dolls. 'Is dinner getting cold…? Ellie, we should go downstairs…'

'We could eat up here.'

'Yes!' Ellie gave him an imploring look and Cass reddened.

'Won't we make a mess?'

'Probably. That's what they make kitchen towel for.' He

met her gaze. Today had changed things. When he'd seen Cass and Ellie together in the classroom window, he'd realised that trying to protect Ellie from Cass's love was not only useless; it was counterproductive. When they'd worked together with Annabel, Jack had wondered just how much else they could achieve together, given the chance.

And Cass had changed too. She'd created a comforting world for Ellie, and it was one that all three of them could share. They hadn't been together like this since he and Cass had slept with Ellie, on his bed, weeks ago.

'I used to have a tent, when I was little.' He smiled at Ellie. 'Grandma used to make burgers and chips, and she'd bring them out to the tent for Grandad and Auntie Sarah and me.'

Two pairs of round eyes gazed at him, Ellie's filled with interest and Cass's with astonishment.

'Auntie Sarah says that my grandad is the same as Ethan's grandad.' Jack realised that Sarah must have talked to Ellie about their father but that he never had, and she was struggling with the concept. It was an omission that he should have rectified by now.

'Yes, that's right. Do you want to see a picture of him? With me and Auntie Sarah when we were little.'

Ellie nodded vigorously.

'Okay. We'll have supper first, though.'

'I'll come and give you a hand.' Cass moved in the cramped space, trying not to knock any of the dolls over.

'It's okay. Stay here.' They didn't need to talk about this. Tonight might be as terrifying in its own way as today had been, but it was long overdue.

They were having fun. The tent that Cass had intended as something to cheer Ellie up with, and would fit only two people and a line of dolls, had turned into a tent for three. Just like a proper family.

Jack had gone to fetch the photograph, disappearing for some time, and Cass supposed it was hidden away somewhere and he'd had to look for it. Ellie had drawn her own version, and Jack had watched thoughtfully.

'He looks like you, Daddy.'

'Yeah. He does, doesn't he?' There was no trace of the anger that surfaced whenever Jack talked about his father. He ran his fingers lightly over the photograph, as if he too were re-drawing it.

'Okay?' Ellie was busy with another picture and Cass ventured the question.

'Yeah. I think so.' Jack still seemed unsure about this, but he'd hidden the tremor in his hands from Ellie. 'You?'

It was nothing to do with her. It was Jack's father, his child, and his conflict...

But when she'd passed Ellie out of the window and seen Jack waiting at the bottom of the ladder, it had felt for a moment as if Ellie was her own child. As if all the pressure and fear were gone, swamped by their shared instincts to keep the little girl safe. Maybe...just maybe...there was some way forward for her and Jack.

'You?' He repeated the question, more pointedly this time.

'Yes. Fine.' Cass turned to the picture that Ellie was drawing, trying to avoid his gaze. 'That's beautiful...'

She'd spoken before she had even looked at the picture. And when she did look, it *was* beautiful. A house. A red crayoned figure who she'd come to recognise as herself, along with a tall figure who could only be Jack. Between them stood four small figures.

'That's me.' Ellie planted her finger on one of the smaller images. 'And Daddy and Cassandra, and my brothers. And that's my sister.'

'Sweetheart...' Jack's voice was strained and Cass couldn't look at him. Didn't dare let him see the tears as her own picture of her perfect family suddenly imploded, smashing itself into pieces.

'That's very nice, Ellie.' She cleared her throat. 'I'm...'

What? Living next door? Coming to rescue Jack and his family? For a moment she couldn't think of any other reason for her to be in the picture than the one that Ellie so obviously intended.

'Okay...' When Jack pulled the picture out from in front of her, she almost cried out with loss. His other arm curled around Ellie and he took her on to his lap for a hug. 'I think it's nearly bedtime, don't you, Ellie?'

'No.' Ellie's voice was indignant.

'I think it is...'

Suddenly Cass couldn't take it. The nightly debate, which Jack always managed to win one way or another. The kiss, before Ellie ran to her father to go up to bed. She squeezed past Jack, almost knocking the tent down in her haste to get out.

'Cass...?'

'I'm going to stack the dishwasher.' She didn't wait for Jack's reply but ran downstairs, turning on the kitchen tap to splash cool water on her face. She'd done the one thing that she'd promised herself she'd never do again. She'd fallen for Jack, and dared to dream about a happy ending. One that could never come true.

Jack tried to get Ellie into bed as fast as he could, but hurrying always seemed to have the same effect. The more he tried to rush, the slower Ellie went. He read Ellie's favourite story, hoping she wouldn't mind that he'd missed a few bits out, listening for any sign of movement downstairs. When he finally kissed Ellie goodnight, the house had been silent for a while.

She was sitting at the kitchen table, nursing a cup of

tea. Cass didn't need to look at him for Jack to know she'd been crying.

'I'm so sorry. She didn't mean it…' The words tumbled out. It was all his fault. If he hadn't talked about his own father, then Ellie would probably never have drawn the picture. Jack had broken his own rule, dared to include Cass in his and Ellie's tiny family unit. And he'd hurt her.

She shrugged. 'I know.'

'She draws whatever happens to be going on in her head at the time. It doesn't mean anything.' He was protesting far too much. Trying to deny the truth. It hadn't just been going on in Ellie's head; it had been going on in his. And, from the look in her eyes, it had been going on in Cass's too.

She shook her head. 'It's what she wants.'

Jack almost choked. 'Ellie has what she needs; this isn't about her.' On that level it wasn't. On another, deeper level, the thought of hurting her the way he'd been hurt, deliberately putting her at risk of losing a parent again, still terrified him.

'No? Then make it about you and me then. How would you feel, knowing that there was no possibility of having any more children?' The intensity in her quiet words made it very clear that they would have been shouted if there wasn't a sleeping child in the house.

'Honestly…?'

She looked up at him suddenly. Such pain in her eyes. 'That would be good. Honesty always is.'

'Honestly, I think it's you that needs to face that, not me.'

'My problem, you mean?' she flared angrily.

'No, I didn't mean that at all. I meant that you're the one who thinks it's a problem in our relationship, not me.'

'We weren't going to have this conversation, Jack. You said you'd keep me safe.'

The words stung because they were true. And wanting to change didn't mean that it was easy.

'It's been a hell of a day. Perhaps we should sleep on it.'

She nodded, her face impassive. 'Yes. I need to be up early tomorrow. I'm seeing the electrician at my house in the morning.'

Jack nodded. 'Are you coming to bed, then?'

He'd never had to ask before. Always known that Cass would go to her own room, to get ready for bed, and then come to his. The moments of waiting, which had seemed like hours in his impatience to hold her, were almost the best part of his day. Second only to when he actually did hold her.

'I don't want to disturb you in the morning. And I could do with some sleep tonight.'

Jack nodded. Saying it out loud had broken the spell. 'I'll see you for supper then. Tomorrow.'

'Yes.' She stood up, bending to kiss his cheek. That, somehow, seemed the most damning thing of all. That she still wanted him, maybe even loved him a little, but there was a gap between them which neither of them could bridge.

He didn't see her again until the following evening. She arrived home late, her face expressionless, and sat down with him in the lounge. Separate chairs, the way they always did, even if there would be no one to see if they curled up together on the sofa. It seemed almost normal, and strangely comforting after having brooded over the possibility that Cass might do what they'd agreed to do all along and take it into her head to call time on their relationship.

'How are things?'

'Fine. Good, actually. The electrician reckons it's safe to restore part of the power supply now, and that means I can get heaters in there to help dry the ground floor out a bit. The motorway's open again.'

One by one, the things that kept her here were disappearing. It was only a matter of time…

'I'm going to move back in.'

Jack swallowed. 'Already?'

'It's easier for me to be there. As long as I have somewhere to sleep, they're still doing lunches and an evening meal up at the church hall.' She pressed her lips together. Clearly she didn't want to talk about it.

'You have somewhere to sleep here.' His bed. In his arms.

'I know.' She sighed. 'But…'

Jack could feel it all slipping away. Protected by secrecy and the four walls of his bedroom, their love affair had blossomed, but as soon as they took it outside that, into the real world, it seemed unbearably fragile.

But maybe, with a little care, it could survive. 'Will you come out with me? One evening. A meal, perhaps.'

She blinked at him. 'You're asking me out on a date?'

'Yeah. I am. Sarah will look after Ellie…'

'I don't think that's a very good idea.'

'Why not?' Okay, so he knew the reasons. Had struggled with the reasons, and Jack still wasn't sure that they weren't valid ones. But surely Cass could give it a try?

'Because…' She stared at him for a moment, her gaze searching his face. 'Because there's no future in it, Jack. I know what it's like to want a child so badly that your whole life seems shattered every time your body tells you that you're not pregnant. I can't go through that again.'

'I'm not asking you to. All I'm asking is that we give it a little time. Find a way to work things out.'

She shook her head, her face suddenly impassive. 'No. That would be too cruel.'

She got to her feet, leaving the room without even looking at him and closing the door behind her in a clear sign that he wasn't to follow her. He heard her soft footsteps on the stairs and the sound of her bedroom door close. Then silence.

Jack stared into the gathering gloom, which had once been a thrilling first hint of the darkness ahead. Now all he could feel was anger. He'd risked everything for Cass, his own heart, and Ellie's. He'd trusted her enough to try to let her into his life but she was still too fearful to even make the effort, and now she was going to leave him.

Maybe she was right and it would never have worked out. And, if that was the case, then he needed to think of Ellie. He needed to protect her.

He sat for a long time, brooding into the darkness, then slumped round on the sofa, fatigue taking over from the what-ifs that were filling his mind. No point in going up to bed. He knew that Cass wouldn't be coming.

Cass was up and packed before there was any sound from Ellie's bedroom. By the time she heard the tinkle of wind chimes heralding the fact that the little girl was awake, she was sitting on the bed in the spare room, staring at the wall.

It was all for the best. This had never been anything other than something temporary, something that couldn't touch their real lives. It had been three weeks since their first night together. Just about the duration of a holiday romance.

The sounds of Jack and Ellie in the bathroom. The smell of breakfast. Everyday things, now tainted with sadness. She waited until she heard Ellie running around in the sitting room, ready to jump on the new day with her customary glee, and went downstairs.

Jack was drowsy and tight-lipped. He closed the kitchen door and turned to her, his face unreadable.

'You're going today?'

'Yeah.'

He nodded. 'Okay. I'm taking Ellie out to the petting

zoo this morning. They've just opened up again after the floods.' His eyes softened suddenly and a thrill of hope ran through her veins. 'Take your time packing.'

Even Jack couldn't fix this. Neither could she. All they could do was to act as if nothing had happened, and that was easy enough. They'd been acting as if nothing was happening practically since they'd first laid eyes on each other.

'I'm ready to go now.'

He nodded abruptly. 'We'll be going soon. Then you can go.'

He couldn't help it. However much he was trying to come to terms with the past, he couldn't do it yet. Jack was cutting her out of his life, another casualty of loss, just like his father and Sal.

'May I…' Cass almost choked on the words. Surely he couldn't be that cruel. 'May I say goodbye to her?'

'Of course.' A glimmer of warmth again in his eyes and then he turned, opening the kitchen door. 'Take whatever time you need.'

It was cold comfort. Cass explained to Ellie that she was going back home today and the little girl nodded, taking it in her stride.

'You're not going far.'

'No, sweetie, not far. You know where I live.'

'That's all right, then.'

Cass hugged her tight, squeezing her eyes closed to stop the tears. Jack called to her from the hallway, persuading her into her coat and wellingtons, and Ellie shouted a goodbye. When Cass went to the front door to wave them off, he didn't even look at her. If Ellie required a hug and a kiss goodbye, Jack obviously required neither.

# CHAPTER EIGHTEEN

THE CLOCK RADIO blared into life and Cass cursed it, reaching out to shut it off. The sudden movement prompted a twinge in her shoulder.

Well it might. She'd been up until midnight last night, putting flat-pack kitchen units together, and they'd been heavier than she'd expected. Today, she might take some time to reflect on the considerable amount of work she'd done on the house in the last two months. Take a few 'work in progress' photographs to compare with the devastation of the 'before' photos and spur her on to the distant date when 'after' photos would be in order.

She took a long shower, still revelling in the fact that she had hot water again. Then padded back to her bedroom, sorting through her wardrobe and on a whim pulling out a skirt. Being able to wear something pretty in the house instead of muddying up her jeans yet again was novelty enough to smack of yet another new achievement.

She made coffee and then went back upstairs to her bedroom, sitting cross-legged on the bed and switching on the television. This was the one room in the house which didn't bear some signs of the devastation the flood had brought with it; downstairs was still a work in progress and the spare room was full of furniture. But here she could relax.

A film maybe. Watching TV on a Sunday morning

seemed like the ultimate luxury. Cass picked up the remote from the bedside cabinet and switched to streaming, flipping through the films on offer. No, not that one. Or that one. Definitely not that; she'd heard it was a weepie. Or that—it was a love story.

The only thing that seemed to drive Jack from her mind was hard work. And the only thing which drove him from her dreams was physical and mental exhaustion. Cass hesitated, looking at her jeans, folded neatly on a chair. Maybe she should put them on and get on with the kitchen cabinets.

The doorbell rang and she climbed off the bed and walked over to the window. Perhaps someone from the village wanted her for something. She almost hoped that it might be a problem which required her immediate attention.

Peering out, she jumped back in horror. Jack's car was parked outside in the lane. Maybe he'd brought Ellie back to renew some acquaintance he'd made here and decided to pop in. Didn't he *know* he couldn't just do that?

Cass watched the front path and saw him stand away from the door, scanning the front of the house. He was alone, and suddenly fear clutched at her heart. Why would he come here without Ellie on a Sunday morning?

She raced downstairs, sliding her feet into her wellingtons when she realised they were the only footwear she had in the hallway. Then she flung open the door.

'Jack...?'

He was making his way back up the path and he turned. Cass's stomach almost did a somersault as suddenly she realised that she hadn't remembered the warmth of his eyes at all. They'd always been so much better in reality.

'What's the matter? Where's Ellie?' Surely the only thing that could bring him here alone was if there was some kind of trouble.

'At Sarah's.' He paused for a moment and then strode back along the path towards her. 'May I come in?'

The temptation to slam the door in his face fought with the need to look at him just a little longer, and lost by a whisker. And she'd opened the door now. Not letting him in would betray the fact that she cared one way or the other.

She stood back from the door in silence and he nodded, wiping his feet and walking into the hall.

'Wow. Quite a difference from last time I saw this.'

Presumably he was referring to the new plaster and skirting boards, and the scrubbed floorboards. All Cass could think about was that the last time he'd been here they'd had something, and now there was nothing.

'It's been hard work.'

'I imagine so.' He seemed a little jumpy. As if there was a point to all of this and he was working himself up to it.

'What do you want, Jack?'

He turned his gaze on her, warm enough to melt chocolate. 'I've come for you, princess.'

No. *No!* What had made him think that he could do this? Leave Ellie with Sarah and pop back for a day spent in bed. Who did he think she was?

'Out.' She glared at him, hoping he'd go before she changed her mind. Her body had just caught on to the idea and was beginning to like it.

'Cass, wait. Can we talk about this?'

'There's nothing to talk about. You can't just drop in whenever you've got a free moment and you think you might like to warm your feet in my bed.'

Reproach flashed in his eyes. 'It's not like that.'

'Okay then, friends with benefits, whatever you want to call it. I'm not interested.'

'Neither am I. Cass, can we sit down…?'

'There's nowhere to sit. The kitchen's full of cupboards, and there's no furniture in the sitting room.' And she wasn't going to take him upstairs to her bedroom.

He rolled his eyes. 'Then we'll do it here.'

'No, we won't. Whatever it is.'

Suddenly he was too close. His lips just an inch away. Cass felt tears begin to roll down her cheeks. 'Jack, stop it. Please...'

'I don't want sex...'

'Stop it!' Didn't he know that friendship was just as much out of the question? She couldn't bear it.

'I want to marry you.'

Suddenly the air began to swim in front of her, distorting everything else. She felt her knees begin to buckle...

Jack managed to catch her before she hit the ground. *Stupid. Stupid.* He shouldn't have just come out with it like that but he was so afraid that Cass was going to throw him out before he got a chance to say it. He settled her in his arms and carried her upstairs, kicking open the nearest door and finding a room stacked with furniture. The other door revealed a large sunny bedroom with light oak furniture and white lace bedlinen.

She was already stirring in his arms and her fingers clutched at his shoulders when he walked over to the bed with her. 'Boots...Jack...'

'Okay. Just relax; I'll take them off.' The room was meticulously clean and tidy, and Jack knew that Cass would probably kill him if he let her wellingtons soil the bed. Sitting her down, he pulled her boots off and then guided her back on to the pillows.

His finger found the pulse in her neck. Strong, even if it was a little fast. His was probably faster.

'I'm all right.'

'I dare say you are. Stay down for a minute.'

She opened her eyes and their pale blue earnestness made his heart lurch. 'I must have just...'

'Have you been eating?' She'd felt light in his arms, and

now that she was lying on her back he could see the line of her hips through the thin fabric of her skirt.

'I…' Her face took on a look of grudging contrition. 'I was putting the kitchen cabinets together last night and didn't stop for supper. I haven't got around to breakfast yet…'

'And so you fainted.' Jack decided not to touch on the immediate reason in case she did it again. He got to his feet. 'Stay there.'

'I'm okay. Really. Just a bit embarrassed.'

Not half as embarrassed as he was, for being such an idiot as to just drop a marriage proposal on her, right out of the blue. But now wasn't the time to mention that, not until she'd had something to eat.

'Stay there.'

'But…'

'No buts, Cass. If you move, I'll… Just don't move.' He tried to put as much authority as he could into his words before he hurried downstairs to the kitchen.

Cass could hear the banging of cupboard doors downstairs. Jack had asked her to marry him?

Maybe she'd got it wrong. Maybe he'd done it on impulse and was regretting it now. Or maybe he'd meant it, and she'd had to go and spoil the moment by fainting. It was her own stupid fault, but the constant hunger for Jack seemed to have overwhelmed everything lately, even hunger for food.

He appeared in the doorway, a glass of milk in one hand and a plate with a couple of croissants in the other. Sitting down on the edge of the bed, he waited for her to sit up before he put the plate on to her lap.

'Feeling better?'

'Yes, much. What were you going to say to me?'

'Eat first.'

How was she going to eat with the words she thought Jack had said bursting in her head like fireworks? She picked up one of the croissants and put it down again.

'I can't.'

He narrowed his eyes. 'Try. C'mon, Cass, I know you can do it.'

'I can't. Really. Jack...' *Please let this be what she thought it was. Please...*

He flashed her a grin. 'I'm glad you can't wait. Don't think I can either.'

'Then get on with it! I'm feeling a little nervous.'

He chuckled. 'Good. I'm feeling a bit nervous too.' Jack picked her hand up from her lap, kissing her fingers, and she nodded him on.

'Cass, you taught me how to believe. And I believe in you. There's only one choice and I've made it. I love you and I want to be with you for the rest of my life. We'll take everything else as it comes, face it together.'

It was everything she wanted to hear. There was only one more question and she had to ask it now, before happiness chipped away at her resolve. 'Are you sure you could be happy? If I couldn't give you children?'

'Wrong question.' He shook his head, smiling. 'If we can't have children *together*, then I can still be very happy. This is how sure I am...'

He reached into his pocket, pulling out a small box. When he opened it Cass clapped her hand to her mouth. The ring inside was beautiful, two diamonds twisted together in a gold setting.

'You're the only woman I'm ever going to want, Cass. You and Ellie are the only family I'm ever going to need. The only question is whether that's enough for you.'

'Me? Are you joking?' He was offering her the whole world and he wanted to know if it was enough?

His mouth curved into a smile. 'I'll let you know when

I'm joking.' He snapped the box shut again and put it back in his pocket.

'Hey! Don't I get to look at it a bit more?'

'I thought you might like to think about it for a while.'

'Jack, ask me again. Please, I know my answer.'

He nodded. He knew her answer too. It had always been this way with Jack. Friends, lovers—they were like two pieces of a jigsaw that fitted perfectly.

He sat on the bed, holding her hands between his. 'Will you marry me, Cass?'

'Yes, Jack. I'll marry you.'

He took the ring out of the box, slipping it on to her finger.


They'd talked for hours, lying together on the bed, side by side. He'd told her his dreams and she'd told him hers. And all of those dreams began slowly to morph into plans.

He was so happy. It felt as if a great weight had been lifted off him, not just the weight of the last months, when he'd struggled to cope without Cass, but the weight of years.

'You want something more to eat?' Jack doubted it. In his remorse at seeing her so thin, he'd raided the kitchen again and she'd worked her way through two sandwiches, a banana and a pot of yoghurt.

'No. I… Were you serious when you said you didn't want sex?' The tone of Cass's voice intimated that she was pretty sure he hadn't been.

'I only want sex under certain conditions.' Her eyebrows shot up and Jack couldn't help smiling.

'Really? Well, you can't just leave me guessing. What conditions?'

'To show how much I love you. To celebrate with you, comfort you, be your companion.' He leaned in to kiss her lightly on the lips, his body burning with need. 'I'm not going to rule out cheap thrills…'

'I like the sound of *cheap thrills*. Would it be quicker to tell me what you *don't* want?'

'Yeah, much.' He eased his leg between her knees. 'I don't want you to be worrying about what time of the month it is, or whether your temperature's just spiked. I want you to see me, Cass. Only me.'

Neither of them had been able to deny that they wanted a child together, but they'd agreed that what they already had was enough. Now was the time to test that out, whether Cass could really leave her own past behind and risk all her broken dreams against what they had now.

'I'd really like that…' She gave him a dazzling smile. 'No expectations, then?'

He wouldn't go quite that far. 'Yeah, I've got expectations. That thing you do… The one that drives me crazy…'

'Which thing is that?'

'Every single one of them. All I see is you, sweetheart.'

'And all I see is you.'

She wound her arms around his neck, pulling him down for a kiss. Then she whispered in his ear, 'Take your clothes off…'

# EPILOGUE

JACK FELT AS if he'd been sitting here for hours, although in truth it was probably only ten minutes. He looked around, towards the entrance of the church, and Mimi elbowed him in the ribs. 'Do that again and I'll be having words with you, Jack.'

'You're supposed to be looking after me, not haranguing me.' Jack had asked Rafe to be his best man and he'd refused, telling him that Mimi was the one he'd crewed an ambulance with for seven years. So convention had been thrown to the wind and both Mimi and Rafe sat beside him.

'She won't be late.' Rafe leaned over. 'Cass is never late.'

'She's already late.'

'No, she isn't.' Mimi looked at her watch. 'She's got another two minutes to go. If you don't stop this, so help me, Jack, I'm going to sedate you.'

A sound at the other end of the aisle. There seemed to be some activity in the porch, and suddenly Ellie appeared. It was the second time in six months that she'd been a bridesmaid and, after the petal-throwing debacle at Rafe and Mimi's wedding, Cass had decided that a sparkly wand might go with the pretty pink dress that Ellie had helped pick for herself.

Ellie waved the wand at the assembled company. Their families, their friends and half the village had turned out and squashed themselves into the church at Holme. Every head turned and the organist struck up the wedding march. This time Ellie didn't take fright and started to walk up the aisle, a look of intense concentration on her face.

Then Jack saw her. She had flowers in her hair and her dress fell in soft folds from an embroidered bodice, emphasising the fluidity of her movements. As Cass walked slowly towards him, her hand resting lightly on her father's arm, he was transfixed.

'Stand up, will you?' Mimi hissed the words in his ear, kicking him. Jack wondered whether his legs would be able to support him. Cass was the most beautiful woman in the world and she'd come here to be his wife.

'You've got the rings?' He turned to Rafe in a sudden panic.

'Of course we have.' Rafe propelled him to his feet and Cass smiled at him. And suddenly everything was not only all right; it was touched with more joy than Jack could ever have imagined one man could stand.

She'd made her vows and he'd made his. As they stepped out of the church and into the spring sunshine, a firefighters' guard of honour stood to attention. Miss Palmer was on the station commander's arm and Ellie capered around, swishing her wand. Everyone trooped across to the village green, where two huge interconnecting marquees had been erected, one to accommodate the buffet and the other for dancing.

Jack was by her side all the way, through the speeches, the cutting of the cake, the excited congratulations. Her soulmate. The hero who had saved her and brought her to a place where she was completely happy.

'Do you have a date yet? For moving in?' Martin beamed at Jack.

'A couple of months, we hope. We're taking our time and doing it properly.'

Both Jack and Ellie loved the house down by the river, and Holme was a good place for Ellie to grow up. They'd chosen the new decorations together and when Jack sold his place there would be cash to build a second storey on to the existing extension if they wanted. Cass found Jack's hand and felt his fingers close around hers.

'And I saw the new wall,' Sue chipped in. 'So, no more repeats of last year.'

'It wasn't all bad. Look what I found washed up on my doorstep.' Cass squeezed Jack's hand and he chuckled.

There was one more thing to be done. Jack had made her feel so happy, so loved, that she'd almost forgotten about monthly cycles and calendars. Until last week. She'd been to the doctor and taken a pregnancy test, just to be sure before she went on her honeymoon.

She'd run all the way home to tell him, stopping just yards from the house. He'd told her that he wanted to marry her without knowing what the future held and she couldn't deprive him of the chance to make that ultimate commitment.

Jack led her on to the dance floor. The weather was warm enough for the walls of the marquee to be removed, leaving just a high domed canopy, strung with lights over their heads. When their first dance was over, other couples started to fill the dance floor.

She felt Jack's chest heave in a long contented sigh and she smiled up at him. 'Happy?'

'I don't think it's possible to be any happier.'

She laughed. 'Sure about that?'

'Positive.'

She stretched up, whispering in his ear.

Mimi was watching the couples on the dance floor as suddenly Jack lifted Cass up, swinging her round. Then he set her back on to her feet again, hugging her tight as tears streamed down his face.

'Look.' She nudged Rafe. 'I don't suppose there's a bit more synchronicity going on, is there…?' It had become a joke between the two couples that Jack had set eyes on Cass at pretty much the same moment that Mimi had seen Rafe again.

Rafe thought for a moment. 'No. I don't.'

'Why not? It makes perfect sense.'

'But what are the odds, Mimi? Seriously. It would be wonderful, but…' His gaze wandered over to where Jack was still hugging Cass.

'Trust me, Rafe. Jack's got that same dazed expression on his face as you had last week, when I told you I was pregnant.'

'Really? I didn't look *that* bad, did I?'

Mimi stood on her toes so she could whisper in his ear. 'You were worse. And much more handsome.'

Rafe chuckled. 'Thank you. Would you like to dance?'

'I'd love to dance.'

\* \* \* \* \*

*If you missed the first story in the*
STRANDED IN HIS ARMS *duet look out for*

*RESCUED BY DR RAFE*

*And if you enjoyed this story,*
*check out these other great reads from*
*Annie Claydon*

*DISCOVERING DR RILEY*
*THE DOCTOR SHE'D NEVER FORGET*
*DARING TO DATE HER EX*
*SNOWBOUND WITH THE SURGEON*

*All available now!*

# MILLS & BOON®
## Hardback – September 2016

# ROMANCE

| | |
|---|---|
| **To Blackmail a Di Sione** | Rachael Thomas |
| **A Ring for Vincenzo's Heir** | Jennie Lucas |
| **Demetriou Demands His Child** | Kate Hewitt |
| **Trapped by Vialli's Vows** | Chantelle Shaw |
| **The Sheikh's Baby Scandal** | Carol Marinelli |
| **Defying the Billionaire's Command** | Michelle Conder |
| **The Secret Beneath the Veil** | Dani Collins |
| **The Mistress That Tamed De Santis** | Natalie Anderson |
| **Stepping into the Prince's World** | Marion Lennox |
| **Unveiling the Bridesmaid** | Jessica Gilmore |
| **The CEO's Surprise Family** | Teresa Carpenter |
| **The Billionaire from Her Past** | Leah Ashton |
| **A Daddy for Her Daughter** | Tina Beckett |
| **Reunited with His Runaway Bride** | Robin Gianna |
| **Rescued by Dr Rafe** | Annie Claydon |
| **Saved by the Single Dad** | Annie Claydon |
| **Sizzling Nights with Dr Off-Limits** | Janice Lynn |
| **Seven Nights with Her Ex** | Louisa Heaton |
| **The Boss's Baby Arrangement** | Catherine Mann |
| **Billionaire Boss, M.D.** | Olivia Gates |

# MILLS & BOON®
## Large Print – September 2016

## ROMANCE

Morelli's Mistress — Anne Mather
A Tycoon to Be Reckoned With — Julia James
Billionaire Without a Past — Carol Marinelli
The Shock Cassano Baby — Andie Brock
The Most Scandalous Ravensdale — Melanie Milburne
The Sheikh's Last Mistress — Rachael Thomas
Claiming the Royal Innocent — Jennifer Hayward
The Billionaire Who Saw Her Beauty — Rebecca Winters
In the Boss's Castle — Jessica Gilmore
One Week with the French Tycoon — Christy McKellen
Rafael's Contract Bride — Nina Milne

## HISTORICAL

In Bed with the Duke — Annie Burrows
More Than a Lover — Ann Lethbridge
Playing the Duke's Mistress — Eliza Redgold
The Blacksmith's Wife — Elisabeth Hobbes
That Despicable Rogue — Virginia Heath

## MEDICAL

The Socialite's Secret — Carol Marinelli
London's Most Eligible Doctor — Annie O'Neil
Saving Maddie's Baby — Marion Lennox
A Sheikh to Capture Her Heart — Meredith Webber
Breaking All Their Rules — Sue MacKay
One Life-Changing Night — Louisa Heaton

# MILLS & BOON®
## Hardback – October 2016

## ROMANCE

| | |
|---|---|
| **The Return of the Di Sione Wife** | Caitlin Crews |
| **Baby of His Revenge** | Jennie Lucas |
| **The Spaniard's Pregnant Bride** | Maisey Yates |
| **A Cinderella for the Greek** | Julia James |
| **Married for the Tycoon's Empire** | Abby Green |
| **Indebted to Moreno** | Kate Walker |
| **A Deal with Alejandro** | Maya Blake |
| **Surrendering to the Italian's Command** | Kim Lawrence |
| **Surrendering to the Italian's Command** | Kim Lawrence |
| **A Mistletoe Kiss with the Boss** | Susan Meier |
| **A Countess for Christmas** | Christy McKellen |
| **Her Festive Baby Bombshell** | Jennifer Faye |
| **The Unexpected Holiday Gift** | Sophie Pembroke |
| **Waking Up to Dr Gorgeous** | Emily Forbes |
| **Swept Away by the Seductive Stranger** | Amy Andrews |
| **One Kiss in Tokyo...** | Scarlet Wilson |
| **The Courage to Love Her Army Doc** | Karin Baine |
| **Reawakened by the Surgeon's Touch** | Jennifer Taylor |
| **Second Chance with Lord Branscombe** | Joanna Neil |
| **The Pregnancy Proposition** | Andrea Laurence |
| **His Illegitimate Heir** | Sarah M. Anderson |

# MILLS & BOON®
## Large Print – October 2016

## ROMANCE

| | |
|---|---|
| Wallflower, Widow...Wife! | Ann Lethbridge |
| Bought for the Greek's Revenge | Lynne Graham |
| An Heir to Make a Marriage | Abby Green |
| The Greek's Nine-Month Redemption | Maisey Yates |
| Expecting a Royal Scandal | Caitlin Crews |
| Return of the Untamed Billionaire | Carol Marinelli |
| Signed Over to Santino | Maya Blake |
| Wedded, Bedded, Betrayed | Michelle Smart |
| The Greek's Nine-Month Surprise | Jennifer Faye |
| A Baby to Save Their Marriage | Scarlet Wilson |
| Stranded with Her Rescuer | Nikki Logan |
| Expecting the Fellani Heir | Lucy Gordon |

## HISTORICAL

| | |
|---|---|
| The Many Sins of Cris de Feaux | Louise Allen |
| Scandal at the Midsummer Ball | Marguerite Kaye & Bronwyn Scott |
| Marriage Made in Hope | Sophia James |
| The Highland Laird's Bride | Nicole Locke |
| An Unsuitable Duchess | Laurie Benson |

## MEDICAL

| | |
|---|---|
| Seduced by the Heart Surgeon | Carol Marinelli |
| Falling for the Single Dad | Emily Forbes |
| The Fling That Changed Everything | Alison Roberts |
| A Child to Open Their Hearts | Marion Lennox |
| The Greek Doctor's Secret Son | Jennifer Taylor |
| Caught in a Storm of Passion | Lucy Ryder |

0916 GEN STD LP